# The Duck who had Goosebumps
### and other Animal Tails

**GRACE FOX ANDERSON** is publications editor of *Counselor,* Scripture Press' take-home paper for children 8 to 11. She has been in church-related work with children for more than 25 years. Mrs. Anderson received her degree in Christian Education from Wheaton College, Wheaton, Ill. Her stories and articles have been published in a variety of Christian magazines. She has also compiled the stories in the popular Winner Books' Animal Tails series: *The Hairy Brown Angel and Other Animal Tails, The Peanut Butter Hamster and Other Animal Tails, Skunk for Rent and Other Animal Tails, The Incompetent Cat and Other Animal Tails,* and *The Pint-Sized Piglet and Other Animal Tails.*

# The Duck who had Goosebumps

### and other Animal Tails

edited by GRACE FOX ANDERSON

illustrated by
Janice Skivington Wood

VICTOR BOOKS ®

A DIVISION OF SCRIPTURE PRESS PUBLICATIONS INC.
USA CANADA ENGLAND

*Third printing, 1989*

**CREDITS:**
"The Duck Who Had Goosebumps," "The Birthday Party," "Bacon for Breakfast," "False Alarm," and "The Great Chicken Enterprise," previously published in, *Action* by Light and Life Press, Winona Lake, IN 46590. "Scat, the Chipmunk," "A Gift for Peter," "The Kitten Club," "God's Gentle Giants," "Run with the Lightning," and "How Winter's Creatures Keep Warm," previously published in *Discovery* by Light and Life Press, Winona Lake, IN 46590. "The Escape of Yellow Eyes," previously published in *Reachout* by Light and Life Press, Winona Lake, IN 46590. "Little Cheese Thief," previously published in *Story Friends* by the Mennonite Publishing House, Scottsdale, PA 15683. "Boots," previously published in *The Christian Leader*, by the Mennonite Brethren, Hillsboro, KS 67063. "Lambie Pie," "Raccoons on the Prowl," "A Place for Everything," "When You Face a Lion," "Pedro and His White Goose," "The 'Talking' Fish," and "The Answer Was Golden," previously published in *Counselor* by Scripture Press Publications, 1825 College Ave., Wheaton, IL 60187.

Scripture quotations in this book are from the *King James Version* (KJV) and from *The Holy Bible, New International Version* (NIV), © 1973, 1978, 1984, International Bible Society. Used by permission of Zondervan Bible Publishers.

Library of Congress Catalog Card Number: 85-62700
ISBN: 0-89693-476-4

VICTOR BOOKS
A division of SP Publications, Inc.
Wheaton, Illinois 60187

# CONTENTS

# The Duck Who Had Goosebumps

*A TRUE STORY*
*by Jane C. Foss*

The two children stepped through the back door of their home into a dazzling fantasy world. During the night, the clouds had dumped icy rain through the chilly atmosphere. As a result, every twig, every surface was coated with a thin sheet of ice. The morning sun had turned the ice to jewels.

"Look, Jan, I can walk on top of the snow." Greg carefully stepped out onto the frozen snow.

"I can stamp through it too," Janet replied as she did just that, making a jagged hole in the crust.

The children made their way to the back of the yard where they could look down the hill through the woods toward the river.

"It looks like a fairyland," Janet said, in hushed tones.

"Like God dropped diamonds all over the woods during the night," Greg added.

Their feet crunched through the snow as they moved down the path to the land below. They followed the path to a wide clearing. Here some of the chunks of ice had broken up and were piled on top of each other. Some of the blocks of ice were as tall as the children.

"It's like mountain climbing. Come on up this one. We can see the river from here," Greg called.

Janet clambered carefully up the icy pile to join Greg at the top. "The river's all ice too," she said.

Sliding down the crust-covered drift, the children continued along the path to the riverbank. For several minutes they moved along the edge of the river, delighted with the shimmering colors made by the sun shining on the icy surfaces.

"It's like the piece of glass Mom bought to hang in the window—you know, the prism. The one with all the little edges that catch the sunlight."

"You're right. Everything here is a prism."

Janet climbed over a slippery log, lost her balance, and fell at the river's edge. As she scrambled to her feet, she cried out to her brother. "Greg, look! Here's a chunk of ice that looks like a duck. It must be a decoy—you know, those wooden ducks hunters use to attract real ducks."

Greg joined her. "It's covered with ice. Let's take it home. I'm getting cold anyway."

Greg picked up the duck, which certainly did look real, and they started the slippery walk back to the house. Climbing back up the hill was not as easy as sliding down had been—especially carrying the duck. Finally, after many slips and slides, they reached the top and hurried into the house.

"Mom, Look! We found a duck down by the river. We think it might be a decoy," Janet cried.

"We want to get the ice off so we can see it better," explained Greg. He put the duck on the work counter in the utility room.

"Be gentle as you take off the ice, Greg," Mother said. "You may take the paint off if you defrost it too fast. Your warm hands will probably be enough to melt the ice."

The children took turns placing their warm hands on the duck. The ice began to melt, trickling off the wings and head in streamlets.

Janet was working on the head. Suddenly her eyes grew larger and she whispered to her brother. "Greg, I think this eye just moved."

Greg pushed her aside and looked more closely at the duck's wet head. "Jan, this is a real, live duck. Mom, come quick! This is a *real* duck! His eye moved."

Dancing with excitement, the children worked faster to melt the ice from the bird. Their mother helped, her larger hands warming more surface. Feathers were visible now. As the ice slid off the wings, the bird began to move and at last was able to lift its wings and shake the remaining ice and water from its body.

"I can't believe it," said Mother. "It must have been sitting near the edge of the river when the sleet started. It was covered before it had a chance to move. You children saved its life."

"Let's get him some food." Greg reached into a bag of cracked corn bought to fill the bird feeders. He placed a handful on the work counter near the duck. The bird scooped up the corn with its bill.

"Let's put some water in the sink in case he wants to swim." Janet ran some lukewarm water into the sink after putting the stopper in the drain. Then they spread out more grain on the counter. The duck continued to eat, then raised his head, shook himself, and jumped into the water.

He fluttered his wings, dipped his head into the water, and began to pick at his feathers.

"He's taking a bath," explained Mother. "I think he's going to be just fine."

"Can we keep him, Mom? We can't put him back outside when the river is frozen," Greg pleaded.

"You're right about that. But I don't think he would be happy inside either," Mother said. "He's a big duck and doesn't look like any I've seen around here. He may have been traveling to his winter home and just stopped here to rest."

"But how can we find out where he belongs?" Janet asked.

"You can make some phone calls. I'll show you where to look in the phone book. We'll leave the duck here," Mother told them.

Closing the utility room door, Mother led the children upstairs to the kitchen and took out the phone book. She gave them a pencil and some paper. Then she showed them which phone numbers to look up in the book. They wrote down the phone numbers for the Division of Wildlife, Parks and Recreation Department, the municipal zoo, and Department of Natural Resources.

"You can take turns making the calls. Just tell whoever answers what has happened and ask if they can help you find out where the duck belongs."

After several calls, the children talked with a man who offered to keep the duck at a game reserve until the weather was clear enough for it to continue its journey. He said the duck did not normally live in the local area but was probably on its way to a wintering place when it was caught in the storm.

The children spent the rest of the day watching the duck.

It seemed content to have them near and showed no fear as they petted its head and stroked its feathers. Late in the afternoon the man from the wildlife reserve arrived and put the duck into a carrying case.

"You children deserve a lot of praise," he said. "You certainly saved this fellow's life. If you hadn't found him and treated him so gently, he never would have survived. As it is, I don't believe he's even lost a feather."

"It would have been fun to keep him," said Janet wistfully as they watched the man put the case into his van.

"But he needs a place to swim and other ducks to be with, Jan," Greg said. "He'd be lonely with just us for friends. I think we did the right thing."

"Mom," began Jan, "do you think God sent Greg and me down the hill this morning to save that duck?"

"That's quite likely, Janet. We're all God's creatures and He works in many ways to take care of us."

Putting an arm around each child, their mother gave them a hug. "Now how about helping me fix some dinner?"

"WANT TO HAVE THE WITS SCARED OUT OF YOU?"

# Fuzzy Teddy Bear

*by Gloria A. Truitt*

Australia is my homeland where
   I live in special trees
Called eucalyptus, and at night
   I eat their tender leaves.
Although I'm not related, I've
   Been called a teddy bear
Because I look just like one with
   My soft and fuzzy hair.
I keep my little ones inside
   My pouch that's snug and warm. . . .
Like any mom, I try to keep
   My babies safe from harm.
Of course, I'm a koala and
   I'm cute as cute can be.
If you should see me in a zoo,
   I'm sure you would agree.

# Scat the Chipmunk

*A NATURE STORY*
*by Judy A. Cross*

I hurried out to see what my cat had. Suddenly, I felt something scurry up my pants leg. When I looked down, a small furry tail was sticking out from under my pants. What was it? I cautiously reached into my pants leg and pulled out a frightened baby chipmunk.

He was so cute and tiny, I decided to keep him for a pet. An old hamster cage suited him fine. He spent most of that day huddled in a corner of the cage. I named him Scat, because he had to scat from the cat.

The next day I found him, motionless, in the same corner. I stuck my hand inside to see if he was OK. He wasn't. He could barely move across his cage.

I carefully took Scat out and wrapped him in a small towel. At first I offered him a piece of barley, but he didn't want it. Then I put some warm milk in an eye dropper and gave that to him. He gobbled the milk down and looked for more.

Instead of milk, I put some honey on a match stick and

**15**

held that out to him. Scat loved it. After he had finished, he began to move around a bit. I put Scat back in his cage—still bundled in the towel. Every few hours I would feed him milk and honey. I hadn't realized that Scat was too little to eat by himself.

Well, Scat made it. By that night he could walk around, but mostly, he liked to nestle in my hand.

Every day I gave Scat his milk and honey. He got to where he started looking for food the minute I picked him up. When I held out the match stick with honey on it, he eagerly took it between his tiny paws and licked all the honey off. Then he would sit in my hand and wash himself.

As the days went by, Scat got more and more friendly. He liked to curl up in the pocket of my overalls while I worked around the house.

I found an old toothbrush, and that became Scat's hairbrush. Every day I brushed Scat's fur until it was sleek and shiny. He seemed to enjoy the brushing. He would lie in my hand and almost go to sleep.

By now Scat could eat on his own. He ate barley, sunflower seeds, corn flakes, potato chips, popcorn, and peanut butter. But his favorite treat was honey.

One day Scat got out of his cage—and did he ever scat! When I wasn't expecting it, Scat would scamper across the floor and zip into another hiding place. It took me several days to catch him. One of those mornings, I felt something nibble on my toes. It was Scat. But when I sat up to see him, he ran off and hid again. I finally caught him when he decided to hide in a towel I laid on the floor.

Now Scat is getting ready for winter. Though he won't be out in the cold, he will still hibernate. I enjoy watching him as he busily totes bits of paper, grass, and string into his house (an empty cocoa can). He is building a bed. He also carries huge amounts of food into his box. Scat looks cute with his cheeks so full of food that they puff out.

Pretty soon Scat will curl up inside his house and go to sleep for the winter. He will only wake up occasionally to eat a bit from his supply.

Sleep well, Scat. See you next spring.

# A Gift for Peter

*A FICTION STORY*
*by Mabel Harmer*

Peter worked carefully as he carved the tiny wooden horses. It was hard to do a good job when his fingers were so
cold. Twice now he had cut a head off a horse entirely and
had started all over again. If it had been an ordinary
carousel, he might have glued the head on again. But this
one had to be perfect. Frau Sommers did not pay for
second-rate work.

He wished that he could stop and warm his hands, but it
was already late, and tomorrow was Christmas. Finally the
carousel was done, and Peter handed it to his father.

"The last one!" exclaimed Herr Franzen. "Now I can
deliver it by nightfall. Perhaps you would like to take it?"

"Yes, Father, I would," replied Peter. "They may invite
me into the great hall where I can see the Christmas tree."

"That is quite possible." His father nodded. "I shall go
out now and buy some gifts for the children." He hesitated
a moment. "What would you like, Peter?"

Peter shook his head. He certainly did not want toys.

After working in the toy shop every day from the minute he was out of school, he was sick of them.

He knew that his mother had knitted new mittens and a pair of socks for each of them. She did that every Christmas. There would be some candies and cakes and perhaps an apple. Well, that was enough for a boy of 10.

His smaller brothers and sisters would expect something more. They liked the toys their father made in his shop. After all, he was the best toymaker in all of Salzburg—or so people said. The children would like the toys until they were as old as Peter and had to help make them.

The toymaker wrapped the carousel carefully and put it in a strong box. "I think this is the finest toy we have ever made," he said. "I hope that the young Sommers children will appreciate it."

"I hope so too," said Peter. He thought of all the hours that had gone into the making of the animals—the horses, the lions, and the zebras. Many times his father had worked late into the night in order to get all of the carving done.

He himself had worked nearly every night after school when he would have liked to have been out on the river, skating with the other boys. Peter put on his shabby coat and cap, wrapping his muffler around his neck so that only his nose and eyes showed.

As his father put the box into his mittened hands, he said, "You will be very careful not to drop it. Perhaps I should go myself."

"Oh, no, Father! You have just an hour before the stores close to buy the Christmas gifts. I can manage."

Just as he reached the door, his father said, "Peter, are you sure you can think of nothing you want for a gift?"

Peter shook his head. Then he smiled. "Don't worry about it, Father. I'll have a good Christmas without any

**19**

special gifts."

Darkness had already fallen upon the city as Peter trudged up the hill to the big house. It was fun to look in the windows. Christmas trees glowed everywhere, and he could see the happy people inside.

He went to the back door of the big house. A maid greeted him, asking, "What is it you want, little boy?"

"This is a gift ordered by Frau Sommers. It was made by my father, Franzen, the toymaker."

"Yes, yes," said the maid. "I'll take care of it."

"Thank you," said Peter. Through an open door he could hear music and laughter. The kitchen table was covered with cakes, nuts, and many other good things to eat. Peter couldn't help thinking that it must be fun to live in a big house and have all of those lovely things.

He took one last look and then turned and went outside. He had gone only a short way when a small brown dog ran up to him and almost jumped into his arms. It was shivering with cold. Peter wrapped part of his muffler around the small creature.

"This is not the time for you to be out in the cold night," he said. "Why don't you go home?"

The only answer was an attempt to nuzzle Peter's neck.

"I wish you were mine," said Peter, rubbing his face against the small brown head. "I would love to have a dog like you. All I ever see are wooden horses and dogs. Not one of them has ever put its head against my cheek."

The dog seemed contented and snuggled down even more closely.

"If I put you down, will you promise to go straight home?" asked Peter. "I am sure someone is worried about you."

He tried, but the dog cried to be picked up again.

"It is late, and I must be on my way home," said Peter. "This is Christmas Eve, you know. I'll try to find your home. Then I must hurry to mine."

Peter couldn't help hoping he would be unsuccessful. He thought he had never seen anything in all his life that he wanted so much. He went to the first house and knocked. A girl came to the door. "Do you know this dog?" he asked.

"No," she said and shut the door.

Peter knocked at three more houses, but no one knew the dog or seemed to care. "I'll make one more call," said Peter. "I'm cold and hungry, and my parents will be worried."

At the last house a lady said, "No, that isn't our dog, but I know where he lives. It's the second house around the corner."

Peter didn't know whether to be glad or sorry. Either way, it didn't make much difference. He took the dog to its home and couldn't help but be glad when a small boy shrieked, "Brownie! O Brownie, where have you been?"

The child's mother came running. "Oh, thank you so much," she said. "It would have spoiled Freddy's Christmas entirely if his dog hadn't been found."

Peter watched the little dog leap joyfully from his arms to those of his small owner. He said good-bye and hurried home.

"What kept you so long?" his mother asked. "We were getting worried about you."

"I knew you would be. I came across a little dog and had to find its home. I almost wished that I hadn't. He was so cute. I wish you could have seen him."

"Yes, all right," said his mother. "Come now and get ready for dinner. It is long past time. The children are eager

**21**

to start."

Their Christmas Eve dinner was a merry time. Afterward they surrounded the tree and sang carols. The children did not need any coaxing to go to bed. The sooner they were asleep, the sooner it would be morning and time to open their gifts.

Peter was tired and ready for bed, but he was not looking forward to gifts, as were the younger ones. He had spoken the truth when he told his father that he wanted no toys.

The next morning he would have stayed in bed for an extra hour if the happy cries of his sisters and brothers had not drawn him downstairs. They were all gathered around the tree looking at their gifts.

"This is for you, Peter," cried Elsa, handing him a new pair of mittens.

"And this!" cried John, giving him a shiny new leather pocketbook.

"And this," came his father's voice from the doorway. Peter turned to see him holding a small brown dog. He jumped to his feet, his face one huge smile.

"How did you get it?" he asked eagerly. "How did you know?"

"From your story last night," answered his father. "I had worried for days what I could give the toymaker's son, who works so hard making toys that he doesn't want any for himself. Then, after you went to bed, I slipped out and got my friend Max to open his pet shop and sell me this dog."

Peter could only murmur his thanks. He took the dog in his arms and let it nuzzle his cheek. This was even better than the dog he had picked up the night before. This dog was his very own.

# The Kitten Club

A FICTION STORY
*by Sharon B. Miller*

"Hi, Kathy," Dawn called as she hurried up the sidewalk to the porch on the front of the big white house.

"Come see the new baby kittens," Kathy called back.

"Oh, they're so cute," Dawn said as she leaned down to look in the box.

Scatter, the gray mother cat, stretched and the kittens squirmed in their sleep.

"There are four of them," Kathy said. "One for you, and one for Gayle, and two for me."

"I'm so glad my mother said I could have one of Scatter's kittens," Dawn said excitedly. "I've wanted a kitten of my own for a long time."

"Gayle wants a kitten too," Kathy said. "Their big black cat got hit by a car last fall."

"Hey, wait for me," Gayle shouted, running down the sidewalk toward them. "Don't pick any out until I get there."

"We're waiting for you," Kathy said as her friend hurried

up onto the porch. "Besides, you and Dawn get first pick. Scatter is mine, so I want you two to take whichever kittens you want."

"Oh, good," Gayle said happily. Then she glanced back out to the street. "Oh, no. She's still following me."

Kathy and Dawn looked up. "Who's following you?" Dawn asked.

"That new girl," Gayle said. "You know—the girl who moved into that shacky house on the street behind our house. My mom was hoping whoever bought it would fix it up. But I don't think these new people are going to. At least that's what my dad said."

"I know which house that is," Kathy said. "My mom said she was going to take some homemade bread to the new people when she baked this week. She's going to invite them to church too."

"I hope she doesn't," Dawn said.

"Why?" Kathy wanted to know. "Everybody ought to go to church to worship God."

Dawn shrugged. "I don't care. I guess it's because she's always got such sloppy clothes. I never see her wearing shoes. Maybe she doesn't have any."

"I could give her some," Kathy said. "I've got an extra pair because my cousin Sandy outgrew her Sunday shoes and gave them to me."

"Let's choose our kittens," Gayle suggested. "Can we hold them?"

"Of course," Kathy said. "Scatter doesn't mind." She picked up the kittens and handed one to each of her friends. She glanced out at the street. The new girl was still standing there, watching them.

"I want this brown-and-white one," Dawn said. "I'm going to name it Fluffy."

24

"And I want this one," Gayle said, putting down the kitten she was holding and taking up a little gray one.

"Hey, I've got an idea," Dawn said. "Let's have a kitten club. We could meet every week and bring the kittens to see Scatter and their brother and sister."

"That sounds like fun," Kathy said. She picked up the gray-and-white kitten and held it up to her face. It meowed and then started to purr as she stroked its soft fur. "I think Scatter would like to see her babies once in a while."

"We could bring the kittens something to eat, and cookies for us," Dawn said excitedly. "What do you think, Kathy?"

Kathy jumped. She hadn't been listening. She was looking out at the new girl still watching them. She looked so sad and lonely.

"What are you doing, thinking about that girl?" Gayle

**25**

asked. "Come on, help us make plans for our kitten club."

Kathy wrinkled her freckled nose in thought. "There is an extra kitten," she said slowly. "There is one kitten left over even after I pick one." She held the little gray-and-white kitten tightly to her and started down the porch steps. She walked right up to the girl standing on the sidewalk.

"Hi, my name is Kathy," she began. "My friends Gayle and Dawn and I are going to have a kitten club. Do you have a kitten? Would you like to join our club?"

"I'm—I'm JoAnn," the girl said shyly. "And I don't have a kitten."

"You can have this one, if you'd like," Kathy said, holding out the tiny furry kitten.

"Oh-h-h!" The girl's eyes got big and bright. "I don't know if my mother and dad would let me have a kitten."

"You could ask," Kathy urged. "Come on. You can see the other kittens and meet my friends. Dawn and Gayle are going to be in the kitten club too. They're also taking Scatter's kittens."

Kathy felt happy as JoAnn followed her up onto the porch. Dawn moved over so JoAnn could look into the box where Scatter lay with her family.

"They're so nice," JoAnn said. "I hope I can have one."

Dawn and Gayle looked at each other. "We do too," they said together.

Kathy laughed and said, "The more in our kitten club, the better. How about coming inside? My mother will let us have milk and chocolate cookies."

Maybe JoAnn didn't have nice clothes or live in a fancy house, Kathy thought as she led the way to the kitchen, but she did need friends. And God would help them make her feel welcome.

# My First Patient

*A TRUE STORY*
by *Nancy F. Sweet-Escott*

All I could think of, talk about, and dream of when I was 10 was horses. I loved all animals, but horses came first. I wanted to be a veterinarian.

My father was a clergyman in a large mining village in England. My brother Jim was interested only in mechanical things and my sister Betty wanted to be a doctor.

My brother and sister laughed at me for wanting to be a vet. However, Mother told me that my grandfather had been a very famous doctor and vet. She even gave me a book of his remedies.

My father was special. I enjoyed being with him. He listened to me. And he loved horses too. Every afternoon I would walk with him around his parish, visiting the sick or going to the coal mines.

One afternoon I was standing with him at the head of a mine shaft, watching the men bring up the ponies that worked in the pits. The poor creatures could be kept underground for only two weeks at a time because the gas lights weakened their eyes.

The ponies were blindfolded when brought up into the daylight. After a day, a hole was punched into their blinders. Each day for about two weeks, the hole was made a little larger. Then it was safe to take the blinders off and turn the ponies out to graze.

As we watched, a little white pony was hauled up. He had dried blood all over his sides and shoulders from sores made by the poorly fitting harness. "Look, Daddy!" I cried. "He is hurt. Can I take him home and make him well? I want him. Please, Daddy?"

Seeing my distress, my father walked over to the owner and asked if we could take the pony home and make him well. The owner was delighted. He said he would bring the pony, whose name was Banjo, to our stables.

Daddy told me I would have to look after Banjo all by myself. "It must not interfere with your studies," he added.

I was so excited. Now I could try my hand at being a vet.

After seeing Banjo put in his new stall, bedded down in deep, clean straw, and contentedly munching on sweet-smelling hay, I got out Grandpa's book of remedies and looked for something to heal Banjo's wounds. But I couldn't find the right remedy.

*I know*, I decided at last. *I'll go to the drugstore and tell Fred* (my friend who worked there) *about Banjo. He will help me.*

Clasping my beloved book under my arm, I hurried down to the drugstore. Fred was kind and helped me pick out the right remedy. Then he gave me the ingredients and told me how to mix and apply them.

I hurried home and took my treasures to my bedroom. Then I ran to the kitchen to get some bowls to mix the medicines in. When I had my medicines all mixed, I took them out to the stable. First I washed the dried blood off Banjo. Then I applied the salve. Who should come by just then but my brother Jim. He looked at me and made some disapproving remarks, but I didn't care. I was doing what I had longed to do.

After two weeks Banjo's wounds were healed and his blinders were due to come off. I removed them carefully.

Banjo had large brown, velvety eyes. When he looked at me as if to say, "Thank you," I fell more in love with him than ever. I was able to turn him out into a paddock with lovely green grass. He couldn't wait to get his head down into it to eat.

I wondered how I was going to catch him to put him in for the night, but he was no trouble at all. That evening I called him and he came galloping toward me and took the apple I had brought him.

I was in seventh heaven looking after him in the days that followed. Finally one day I said to myself, "Why shouldn't I get on his back and ride him?" I didn't want to ask anyone's help, so when he was eating with his head down, I carefully put my right leg over his neck. He immediately lifted his head and I slid down onto his back.

Every day I did this and, as he got stronger, he would gallop around the field. Sometimes he cut the corners sharply and I tumbled off. Then he would come back and stand by me and put his head down and wait for me to get on his back. Then off we'd go for another gallop.

One day his owner came to see how Banjo was. When he saw how well the pony looked, he said Banjo must go back to work. He tried to catch Banjo, but the pony would have no part of him. The owner shook his head and gave up but reappeared with three helpers. They cornered Banjo several times but somehow the pony managed each time to escape them. Finally they asked me to catch him.

"Let him settle down a bit," I said. "Then I will catch him. But you must hide."

Fifteen minutes later, when Banjo was grazing contentedly, I went out with the halter behind my back. Banjo was suspicious, so I kept talking to him, telling him how much I loved him only he had to go back to work for a while, then he could come back again. Finally I got him, climbed on his back, and rode him triumphantly into the yard.

I cried when Banjo left. As I stood there, hoping he understood what I had told him, my brother came up. He had been watching and said, "Maybe you should be a vet, Nancy. You certainly have a way with a horse. I won't laugh at you anymore."

His kind words helped relieve my sorrow at losing Banjo. From then on, Jim and I were friends again. Only Betty still laughed at me. But with Jim plugging for me, I felt greatly encouraged. Someday, I was sure, I would be a vet.

As it turned out, I became a horse trainer instead and loved my years of working with these four-footed friends.

# God's Gentle Giants

## A NATURE STORY
### by Sharon B. Miller

People first called them the Great Horses. They were very large and strong. During the Christian Crusades of the 11th, 12th, and 13th centuries, knights rode these giant horses into battle.

It was important for a knight to have a big horse. The knight wore heavy armor for protection when he went into battle. The armor weighed so much that the knight often had to be lifted onto his horse by a crane. It took a strong horse to carry such weight. If the knight was knocked off his horse or fell off while fighting, he was unable to get to his feet alone and was at the mercy of his enemy.

A Great Horse or *Percheron* carried Joan of Arc when she led her army to battle. Percherons are large, dapple-gray or black horses. They come from Perche, France. A farmer from Illinois, named Wayne, brought the first Percherons to America in 1839.

Several kinds of draft or work horses take their names from the areas of the country where they are raised. The

*Shire* from England is the biggest work horse. You can recognize him by the large feathers around his feet and lower legs. He is almost six feet tall at the top of his shoulder. He often weighs more than a ton—up to 2,300 pounds. But because he is so big, the Shire doesn't have much energy. However, when he works, he accomplishes a lot. He can pull as much as five tons or 10,000 pounds.

King Henry the Eighth, of England, issued a law that said any Shire less than 15 hands high had to be destroyed. (A hand is four inches.) Since England's pastureland was limited, the king wanted only the biggest horses. By allowing only the largest to live and reproduce, they got even bigger horses.

The most popular draft horse is the *Clydesdale*. He is the national horse of Scotland. He also has feathers at his hocks and feet but is daintier looking than the Shire. You can recognize the Clydesdale by the white markings on his face and legs.

Before the automobile, the Clydesdale was a common sight in cities. He was a smart-looking, classy horse. People liked him to pull their carriages. Today, you may see several teams of Clydesdales hitched together, pulling wagons in parades.

The *Belgian* horse from Brussels weighs about a ton, or 2,000 pounds. You can see a team of these beauties at pulling contests in country areas. A good team can pull four times their weight. Belgians are popular and can often be seen pulling in fields today.

Seldom seen is the *Suffolk* (from Suffolk, England). The smallest draft horse, the Suffolk is gentle and works willingly. He is always chestnut color, but comes in many varieties. He is noted for his good trot.

Before people had cars and tractors, more work horses

than riding horses were used. They pulled plows, wagons, carriages, street cars, milk wagons, and sleighs, and hauled logs in the forests and cleared fields of stumps. All heavy work was done by horsepower.

Having a good horse often meant the difference between a man making a good living for his family or being very poor. Men took better care of their horses than they did of themselves. They prided themselves on their horses' condition, ability, and training. After a hard day in the fields, before the farmer went to the house to eat and rest himself, he would make sure his horses were fed, watered, and brushed down.

Riding horses are often flighty and excitable. But when God created the work or draft horse, He gave him a gentle nature which makes him easy to handle. Some draft teams are so gentle and obedient that a small boy can harness and drive them alone. Some are so well trained they will work by voice command with no one holding the reins. They simply obey their master's command, "Giddup," or "Whoa," or "Gee" (turn right) or "Haw" (turn left).

When farmers began to use tractors widely, people lost interest in the draft horse. Because they are often called work horses, they did not seem as exciting as the prancing, riding horses. While they can be ridden, they are not as fast or comfortable as the smaller riding horses.

But in recent years, people have begun to show an interest in big horses again. They are discovering that draft horses are not only big but are beautiful and exciting to own. Draft horse shows and auctions where only draft horses are sold are becoming more popular.

People who want to live a simple life are using draft horses to plow their fields and gardens much as people did long ago. Some people just enjoy raising draft horses. Draft colts are beautiful babies. In months, they grow bigger than some riding horses. If you look, you may see these big horses working in fields or pulling wagons around where you live.

You won't see a prettier sight than a well-groomed team of draft horses trotting down the street in a parade with their harnesses gleaming. They remind us that God's creatures can indeed be beautiful as well as helpful to us. When the Lord made the gentle, giant draft horse, He created an animal that has brought a lot of pleasure and comfort to people.

# Shaggy Mountain Climber

*by Gloria A. Truitt*

My shaggy hair is white and coarse,
　　My watchful eyes are yellow.
And though my walk is slow and stiff,
　　I'm not a lazy fellow.
Eagles, wolves and foxes are
　　The enemies I fear,
But I can gallop, run, and leap
　　Much faster than a deer!
Although I live in regions that
　　Are rocky and remote,
There is no finer place for me,
　　'Cause I'm a mountain goat!

©1986 Gloria Truitt

# Lambie Pie

*A TRUE STORY*
*told by Tom Houvenagle*
*Written by Shirley Houvenagle*

Every time I see the small white collar with a silver bell on it, I think of Lambie Pie. You see, my own woolly lamb once wore that collar. But now it hangs on a peg in the sheep barn.

I remember the rainy Saturday when I first saw Lambie Pie. Dad had taken my brother and me to the sheep sale barn the week before just to watch. This time, however, we were actually going to buy some lambs for our 4-H project. We listened carefully, trying to understand the auctioneer.

Finally, one woolly little lamb bounded into the ring alone. She bleated pitifully. Her big black eyes looked right at me. I pulled on Dad's sleeve. The bidding began.

"Who'll give me ten?" called the auctioneer. "Who'll give me ten? Ten? Ten? Right there. Who'll give me ten and a half? Ten and a half?"

It seemed the bidding was going higher and higher. I shut my eyes and prayed. When at last I opened them, the bidding had stopped and the auctioneer was pointing at

Dad.

"Sold to the gentleman in the red coat," the auctioneer said. "What's your name, sir?"

After a time Dad bought four larger lambs that came into the ring together. However, I was more excited about the cute little black-faced one than all the others.

We pulled the lambs home in our canvas-covered trailer. Then we unloaded them into our pasture. We had worked hard, getting the fences ready for the sheep.

My brother and I talked a lot about what we would do with them. We dreamed of having a large flock of sheep some day. When these lambs grew up and had lambs of their own, we would keep them all. The next year we would have even more. We read books about the care of lambs and what they should eat.

Every day we would go out to the pasture and look them over. The little black-faced one would walk right up to us. We started calling her Lambie Pie because she was so special. Dad even bought a collar with a silver bell on it for her to wear. He said it would make the lambs easier to locate in the evenings when it was time to put them in the barn.

I noticed the other lambs all seemed to stick together. When Lambie Pie would walk up to them, they would butt her and push her away roughly. I knew just how she felt for I had just changed to a new school. Sometimes the kids at school treated me the way the four lambs treated Lambie Pie.

I guess that's one reason I liked her so much. I felt sorry for her and knew what she was going through. But she never complained. She just walked along behind the bigger lambs with her head down as if she were grazing.

Then, one Sunday, my grandmother came out from the

city. I took her out to see how fat the lambs were getting. Lambie Pie wasn't with the others. We looked around and listened. At last we heard a faint tinkle coming from some tall weeds. She must have crawled in there to hide because she felt sick. I tried to get her up but she was too weak to walk. We had to carry her back to the sheep barn.

Dad came out and looked her over. He thought she had pneumonia. He called a veterinarian and got some medicine for her, but Lambie Pie never walked again.

While she was sick, I remembered that she never seemed to eat anything and I asked Dad if he couldn't call the people who used to own her to see what they had fed her.

It was then we found out that she had been an orphaned lamb. Another boy had raised her on a bottle. She wasn't eating enough other foods to be taken off milk so had slowly starved. She had caught cold because she was weak. Right away I began feeding her warm milk in a bottle but she was too sick to drink much.

I felt sorrier than ever for her. Even her own mother hadn't been able to care for her!

When I got home from school, I carried her out and put her under the apple tree. Sometimes I'd sit beside her and pet her ears. Her eyes were always quiet and gentle. I loved her so much.

Mother brought out her Bible once and read to me from Isaiah. It described the Lord Jesus "as a Lamb to the slaughter, and as a sheep before her shearers is dumb, so He openeth not His mouth" (Isaiah 53:7, KJV)). When I had memorized that verse a year or two earlier, I had no idea what it meant. Now I do.

I thought too about how the Lord is our shepherd and we are like sheep (Psalm 23). We are helpless without God, but He takes care of us just right if we let Him. It made me glad that I belong to God. I accepted Jesus as my Saviour at Bible Club in the town where we used to live.

I prayed every day that Lambie Pie would get well. However, one morning before I went to school mother came up to my room. "Lambie Pie died in the night," she said.

I knew then that for some reason, it wasn't God's will for the lamb to live. At least her suffering was over.

Before I went to school, I buried her out beside the garage. My heart ached with every shovel of dirt. I'll never forget how she used to look with her woolly black face and floppy long ears.

For awhile, I didn't care much about the other lambs. Mother said God knew when we bought Lambie Pie what would happen. He had a lesson to teach us through her gentle ways, perhaps a lesson about Jesus, who said, "I am the Good Shepherd, and know My sheep."

The other four lambs are grown-up sheep now and soon will have lambs of their own. My brother and I hope that one will look like Lambie Pie. If it does, it too will wear the little white collar with the silver bell and have the name "Lambie Pie."

# A Place for Everything

## A TRUE STORY
### by Gloria A. Truitt

It was a beautiful June morning. *What a perfect day for a walk in the woods*, thought 10-year-old Johnny Truitt as he looked out the window at a robin, hopping around in the dewy grass. Maybe, just maybe, his parents would agree.

Johnny hurried out to the kitchen where his mother and father were finishing breakfast. "Since you have a day off work today, Dad, could we go for a hike along Carp River?" he asked.

His father smiled. "I don't see why not," he said.

Mom packed a picnic lunch and they were soon in the car and on their way. After a few miles, father found the twisting, dirt road that led to the mouth of the Carp River.

From deep within the forests of northern Michigan, the river flowed lazily through a wooded valley, out to Lake Superior. Dad parked the car near a flat bank where the river was wide and calm. The late morning sun glistened from the water's glassy surface. Here and there, birds darted from branches overhead. And crickets chirped with the frogs who sat hidden in the rushes.

"God created such a beautiful world," sighed Johnny's mother as she walked along the river's edge, admiring the wild violets and primroses.

"Yes," answered Dad. "God certainly has put everything in its perfect place, even the rocks and flowers."

Johnny ran ahead and found just the right spot for their picnic. He set the basket down on a large patch of soft grass that reached almost to the water.

While waiting for his parents, he knelt at the edge of the river and watched water bugs skate across the surface. Suddenly, a dark shadow appeared in the water. It moved like an inky cloud, and Johnny was curious. He almost fell in as he leaned over for a closer look. "They're minnows!" he yelled, and dashed to the picnic basket for a paper cup.

Dad hurried to his side as Johnny dipped the cup beneath the surface. "Look! Thousands of them!" he said as he drew the cup out of the water.

"Take another look," his father said laughing. "They're *not* minnows."

Johnny peered into the cup and noticed that each tiny "fish" had two front legs. "But fish don't have legs. Yippee! They're tadpoles!" Johnny cried.

Without spilling a drop, he carried the cup to where his mother was spreading the tablecloth. "I've always wanted to raise a frog," he said, "and, wow, do I have a lot of them!"

Mom and Dad peered into the dark mass of swimming tadpoles. "I really think you should leave them here," said Dad. "Tadpoles are hard to raise."

"Aw, I'll take good care of them," Johnny begged.

"But what will you do with 30 frogs?" Mom asked.

"That's no problem," Johnny said. "After they've grown

**41**

we'll bring them back here!"

"All right," his father agreed. "We'll let you try, but I don't think it's a good idea."

After the family returned home, Johnny dumped the tadpoles into a big shallow bowl, along with some extra river water. Then he placed a few rocks in the bowl so they could climb up and breathe air as they developed into frogs.

"What about their food?" Mom asked.

"Hmmm, I hadn't thought about that," Johnny said. "What do they eat?"

They learned from a book that after a tadpole's front legs appear, it doesn't eat until it becomes a frog. "Well," said Johnny, "that solves the food problem."

Early the next morning, Johnny ran out to visit his bowl of tadpoles on the patio. In less than a day, little hind legs had emerged. Although most of the tadpoles swam in the

shadow of the rocks, several had already climbed out of the water to rest on the stones.

A moment later Johnny heard his friends calling. He forgot about the tadpoles and left to join his friends for a game of basketball at the park. The day grew hot. Finally Johnny wiped his forehead, saying, "Whew! I quit! Come home with me and see my tadpoles."

As soon as he looked into the bowl, he knew something was wrong. At least half of the tadpoles were drifting lifelessly on the bottom. "They're dead!" he cried. "And they were swimming around like crazy this morning!"

The shallow bowl had not provided enough shade for the mass of tadpoles. As the temperature had risen, only those that had found shade near the rocks had lived.

"Too bad you lost so many," said one of Johnny's friends. "But the rest seem to be OK."

"Yeah," Johnny said doubtfully. "I sure hope so."

After his friends went home, he decided to put the bowl on the back porch. The tadpoles would be safe from the hot sun there and he could keep a closer watch on them.

At bedtime the remaining 12 tadpoles were still alive. In fact, they seemed to be changing right before Johnny's eyes. Since morning their tails had actually become shorter!

Before breakfast the next morning, Johnny ran out to the porch and looked into the bowl. *One—two—three. Where are the rest of the tadpoles?* he wondered. He stuck his finger into the bowl and gently stirred the rocks, but the tadpoles were not hiding.

"My tadpoles disappeared!" he shouted.

Dad carried his coffee cup to the porch and peered over Johnny's shoulder. "I guess they did!" he said in surprise.

"Hurry and find them!" Mom said. "They're probably hopping around my kitchen!"

Everyone looked, but Johnny was the one to find them. They lay still and shrunken on the porch floor. Quietly Johnny said, "They're not hopping. They're dead."

"Oh dear, what went wrong this time?" his mother asked.

"They jumped out of the bowl," said Dad. "When they couldn't get back in, they dried up from lack of water."

"I only have three left," said Johnny sadly.

"And I think we'd better take them back to the river right now—*before* they become frogs," Dad said.

Johnny glanced at the tadpoles, then back at his father. "I guess you were right, Dad," he sighed. "They *are* hard to raise."

A short time later, Johnny watched as the last three tadpoles swam off and vanished into the weeds along the river. "Well, at least three lived," he said. "No thanks to me."

"You've learned a hard lesson," his father said. "We must respect all forms of life—even tadpoles."

When they got home, Dad took out his Bible and read some verses to Johnny. "So God created the great creatures of the sea and every living and moving thing with which the water teems, according to their kinds. . . . And God saw that it was good. God blessed them and said, 'Be fruitful and increase in number and fill the water in the seas' " (Genesis 1:21-22, NIV).

When his father had finished, Johnny looked up with a smile. "Now I know what you meant the other day when you said that God puts everything in its perfect place."

# Pedro and His White Goose

*A TRUE STORY*
*by Theresa Worman*

Pedro Hernandez pushed his hands into the pockets of his jeans and kicked up little clouds of dust with his bare feet. His hat flopped up and down and his teeth glistened in the sunlight as he sang a song he had made up. He was singing to a big white goose, waddling slowly behind him:

> Rudolpho has a barking dog;
> Maria has a stubborn mule;
> But Pedro has a big white goose
> That goes with him to Sunday School.

The big white goose kept nodding her head. She seemed to say, "How foolish to have a barking dog or a stubborn mule for a pet when you can have a beautiful goose like me!"

Pedro lived with his mother and three sisters in a white-washed house in Mexico. Once in a while his father came home for a week or two. But he was gone most of the time because he worked in the faraway mines.

Mama Hernandez took good care of the house Papa had built. She kept it clean and tidy. Bright flowers bloomed in the yard.

One day Señorita Marietta, who helped missionaries at the little white church down the road, had come to Pedro's home. She had read to Pedro, his mama, and sisters from the Bible. They had never seen a Bible close up before.

Señorita Marietta read how God loved them so much that He sent His Son, the Lord Jesus, from heaven to die on a cross for them. She told Pedro and his family that God wanted them to love His Son Jesus and accept Him as their Saviour. They all listened politely as the señorita talked.

When she had finished, Pedro said quietly, "The Lord Jesus—He is good to die for Pedro. I love Him, Señorita."

But Mama Hernandez would not say she loved the Lord Jesus. And because she would not say so, neither would Maria nor Angelica nor Rosa.

Señorita Marietta gave Pedro her Bible for his very own. She showed him where he could read about the dear Lord Jesus dying for his sins and rising from the grave.

"I am so glad that you belong to the Lord now, Pedro," she said. "But I am sad because your mama and sisters will not believe."

Pedro was glad and sad too.

After that day when he had received Jesus as his Saviour, Pedro went to Sunday School every Sunday morning. Mama would not go with him, neither would Maria nor Rosa nor Angelica. But Pedro did not go alone. He took his pet goose with him.

Each Sunday morning Pedro would ask, "Mama, will you come with me to Sunday School? Will you come and hear the nice talk about Jesus and the pretty singing?"

But Mama would always say, "Your mama has no time, Pedro. I must cook the beans, scrub the floor, and wash the clothes. Take your goose and run along. Do not bother me. I'm busy."

Sometimes Pedro would beg his older sister, Maria, to go with him, but she did not like to sit still and listen to the señorita tell stories from the Bible. "You go to Sunday School, Pedro," she would say. "I will stay home and play with Angelica and little Rosa. You and your goose go to Sunday School."

Señorita Marietta talked with Pedro's mother several times. She said, "It is lonesome for a boy to go to Sunday School with only a pet goose for company. God expects mothers to teach their children about Him."

Mother Hernandez would sigh and say, "Poor Pedro! He is such a good boy since he goes to Sunday School. Maybe I will go sometime too." But she never did.

Each Sunday when Pedro and his goose reached the church, Pedro would take a long string out of his pocket. He would tie one end to the goose's leg and the other end to the castor bean tree in front of the little white church. Then he'd take a handful of grain out of his pocket and sprinkle it on the ground. The goose was happy pecking at the grain while it lasted, and Pedro was happy in Sunday School.

Nearly every Sunday Señorita Marietta would be outside, watching for Pedro. "And how is your goose today?" she would ask.

"She is fine, Señorita," he would reply. "She likes to come to Sunday School."

"She likes to come because you have brought her here since she was young," the señorita said.

"Always I am asking Mama and my sisters to come,"

Pedro would say. "But they do not want to."

"It is too bad, Pedro," Señorita Marietta would sympathize. "But you know the dear Lord Jesus often had to be alone when He was here on earth."

"And He didn't have a nice pet goose, did He, señorita?" Pedro said seriously one Sunday.

"No," she answered smiling. "You and your goose keep coming. Your mama and sisters are watching to see if you are good because you love Jesus. Keep on asking God to make your mama want to come.

"God will hear your prayer and answer, though I don't know how or when."

The following Sunday Señorita Marietta was surprised. Pedro arrived without his goose. "Why, Pedro," she gasped. "Where is your goose?"

"Oh, it is wonderful!" he exclaimed. "The goose is to be a mama. At home she sits on five big eggs. She won't leave them even to come to Sunday School."

In fact, the goose was very cross and hard to get along with during those days when she sat on the eggs. Pedro took special care of her, but even he could not get too close to her nest.

One day when Pedro was walking lazily home from school, Maria came running down the road to meet him with her black braids flying. "Pedro! Pedro!"she screamed. "The goose; the goose!" Maria was so out of breath she couldn't say any more.

Thinking something terrible had happened, Pedro ran past Maria, as fast as he could. But there in the backyard stood Mama and Angelica and Rosa. And there was the goose, prouder than she had ever been before. For close beside her were three little yellow goslings!

Whenever he could after that, Pedro watched the goose

and her little ones.

On Sunday morning Pedro asked, "Mama, you will come to Sunday School and hear about Jesus?"

"Not today, Pedro. Mama has to make tamales. You run along."

So Pedro started off, glad to go to the house of God, but sad because he had to go alone. He had almost reached the road when he heard a noise behind him. He looked back and there were Mama goose and her three goslings.

Mama Hernandez was standing in her doorway. She saw Pedro going down the road with Mama Goose and her three goslings walking behind him—all on their way to Sunday School.

"Well," she said, with her hands on her hips. "I will not have it said that a goose takes better care of her children than I do. If a goose can take her family to Sunday School, so can I."

"Pedro! Pedro!" she called. "Come quick!"

"What's wrong, Mama?" Pedro called.

"Pedro, Mama is going to Sunday School. Get Rosa. Here, Angelica, wash your face and comb your hair. Maria, get yourself cleaned up nice. Quick! Quick! We are all going to Sunday School."

Señorita Marietta stood on the steps of the white church that morning. She blinked her eyes, for she could hardly believe she was seeing right. Down the road came Pedro, proud and happy. Behind him came Mama Hernandez with Maria, Angelica, and Rosa. And behind Rosa waddled Mama Goose and her three little yellow goslings.

**49**

# Big Mouth

### by Gloria A. Truitt

Sometimes I look just like a log
   While dozing in the sun.
But if my jaws go *snap, snap, snap,*
   You'd better start to run!

The salt marshes of Florida
   And 'long the river, Nile,
Are *home sweet home* to me for I'm
   The vicious crocodile!

**50**

# The Birthday Party

*A FICTION STORY*
*by Geraldine Nicholas*

"But Mom," Julie objected. "I don't *want* to invite Corinne to my birthday party." Her voice sounded whiney and impatient. "I don't mind her coming over here sometimes to play, or even taking her along when we go on a picnic. But not to my birthday party. She'll spoil everything. And she'll have to bring along that big, ugly dog!"

"But, Julie," her mother interrupted. "I thought Corinne was a good friend of yours. She'd be hurt if she knew you were having a party and didn't invite her."

"I don't *want* her," Julie insisted as she pushed angrily past her mother and ran upstairs to her bedroom. She slammed the door hard and plunked herself down on her bed. The mirror at the end of the bed reflected her angry, red face.

*How can Mom be so mean? She expects so much of me.* "Well, I guess I can invite who I want to my own party," she mumbled indignantly. "And I *don't* want Corinne Cooper!"

Julie leaned back on her pillow and shut her eyes. She knew Corinne couldn't help it that she was blind. But it wasn't Julie's problem either. And she didn't want her making everyone feel uncomfortable at her party. Lisa might understand her being so different, but Janice and Dee Dee would be sure to laugh at the way Corinne blinked all the time. And they'd think Julie was stupid to invite her.

All during supper, Julie waited for her mother to tell Dad how she had acted. She was surprised when Mom didn't mention her behavior. Finally, when her mom was dishing out dessert, Julie blurted out, "All right, Corinne can come to my party! But my friends aren't going to like it. I'm going to feel pretty embarrassed, but I'll invite her since you want me to, Mom," she added, frowning. Her mom and dad exchanged glances but neither said a word.

The next day Julie put Corinne's invitation in her mailbox. In the evening, Corinne called to say she could come.

Julie didn't mention to Lisa, Janice, or Dee Dee that Corinne was coming to her party. When they arrived, they were surprised to see her sitting in the big rocker in Julie's bedroom with her collie Simba, stretched out at her feet.

Because Corinne was listening to some records, she didn't hear the girls come in until Dee Dee snickered. When Corinne turned toward them, it seemed as if she could see. They all felt pretty uncomfortable.

"Julie," Corinne asked, "is everyone here for the party?"

Julie's face flushed. She looked at her friends and shrugged. "Everybody's here, Corinne," she said. "Dee Dee, Janice, and Lisa."

They all said "hi" to Corinne. Then she suggested that Julie open her presents.

Janice gave Julie a T-shirt that said "Let's be Friends" on the front. Lisa gave her a record and Dee Dee's gift was a large puzzle. Julie opened Corinne's gift last. It was a brown, leather dog collar with *Char* for Charley engraved on the attached metal plate. Printed under his name were Julie's address and telephone number in small letters.

"How did you know Char needed a new collar?" Julie asked.

"I could tell he'd lost his collar last week when I was sitting out front," Corinne told her. "Char comes over a lot when you're away. He and Simba get along pretty well. I missed feeling the collar on his neck so I asked your mother about it. She said he'd lost it and that you were planning on getting him another one. I thought it would be a good birthday present. I'm glad you like it."

"I love it," Julie said, "and so will Char."

"Want me to go and get him?" Janice asked.

"Yeah. Let's see if it fits. He's probably down in the kitchen."

Janice was back in a few minutes with Char. The collar fit perfectly. He strutted around the room modeling his new collar, then lay down on his special mat next to Julie's bed.

Later, Julie's dad took them all bowling. Of course, Corinne didn't bowl, but she sat on the sidelines and cheered them along. Julie's mom had a birthday supper ready for them when they got home. No one paid much attention to Corinne's handicap by then. She had a good sense of humor and kept the girls laughing all during supper. She even told jokes about her own blindness, which made them all relax. Like when she asked, "What has eyes and can't see—just like me?" None of them could guess, so Corinne told them, "A potato!"

It wasn't until everyone had gone home and Julie was

getting ready to take a shower that she missed Char. She put on her robe and went outside to look for him. She called him but he didn't come. *Strange,* she thought. *He's never gone away like this before.*

Julie told her dad that she couldn't find Char, but he didn't seem concerned. "He won't be far away," he chuckled. "He'd never find another family who would spoil him like we do. Don't worry, Julie. He'll be back. But you'd better be getting to bed. It's way past your bedtime."

When her mother came in to say good-night, Julie asked her to check outside again before she went to bed. Her mom assured her too. "Don't worry, Dear. He isn't far away. It's not cold out tonight anyway, even if he does stay out all night."

"Mom," Julie called just before she left the room. "I'm glad Corinne came to my birthday party."

Her mother just smiled and turned out the light.

Julie awoke to a beautiful June Sunday morning with the sun streaming through the window. She sat up to see if Char was lying in his usual place next to her bed. But he wasn't there.

Grabbing her robe, Julie jumped out of bed and ran downstairs. Char was nowhere in the house so she went out to the yard, looking and calling. No sign of him anywhere.

Something was wrong. She just knew it. She dashed upstairs to tell her mom and dad. "He's still gone," she shouted as she opened their bedroom door.

Her dad opened one sleepy eye. "Who's gone?" he mumbled drowsily.

"Char's still not home, Dad! We've got to *do* something. Something's wrong. I know it!"

Her dad sat up in bed and looked over at the clock. "Six-thirty," he mumbled. "It's too early to do anything yet, Julie. You go back to bed for a while and then we'll talk about it."

"But Dad, I know something's wrong. Couldn't we do something *now?*" she insisted.

"If he's not back when we get home from church, we'll start searching. Now go back to bed," he ordered.

*Poor Char,* she thought as she crawled back into bed. She lay there imagining all kinds of things that could have happened to him. Like being run over by a car and lying in the road all night in pain. Every once in a while there was something in the newspaper about an animal in the area being found poisoned. Just thinking of it made her shiver.

Julie remembered her dad reading the verse from the Bible during devotions a few weeks ago—"You do not have, because you do not ask God" (James 4:2, NIV). He said that God wanted us to talk to Him about everything. So Julie crawled out of bed and knelt on Char's mat to ask God to help them find the dog.

It was very hard for her to concentrate on what went on in Sunday School and church that morning. When they got home, after church, Corinne was sitting on her front steps next door. Simba was at her feet as usual.

When Julie got out of the car, Corinne called to her to come over. She said she had something important to tell her. "There was a truck here from the animal shelter about an hour ago," she told Julie. "The man gave Mom a phone number for you to call. I have it here." She handed a piece of paper to Julie.

Julie's heart leaped. There was a short message scrawled on the paper. "Call Jason at 850-0241. Delta Animal Shelter."

"Thanks, Corinne. Thanks a lot," Julie said as she

dashed across the lawn and into her house. Her dad phoned Jason, and sure enough, Jason had found Char. The dog's foot had been caught under a barricade that had fallen at a construction site only a block from their house.

Char had been pinned under it for a long time, "Maybe even all night," Jason said. Char was all right except that his right front foot had been badly injured when a nail had gone through it. They had treated him at the animal shelter for infection and had wrapped the wound.

"When did you find him?"

"About mid-morning," Jason said. "Maybe 10 o'clock. We couldn't reach you so we treated him with antibiotics. The foot was quite swollen and infected and we didn't know how long the nail had been in it. We don't usually treat animals without contacting their owners first, but because of the collar he was wearing, we felt sure he must be a dog with a family that cared about him."

It was Corinne's collar that had saved Char. Julie was sure of it. She ran right over to tell her and to thank her again for the gift. She invited Corinne to go along with them to pick Char up at the animal shelter.

Char was excited to see his family again. He could still jump up, even with the injured foot. He sprang wildly from one to the other. If he was in any pain, he didn't show it.

Lisa and Dee Dee dropped by while Corinne was there. And Julie was proud to tell them that Corinne's birthday gift had helped find her dog. And always after that, she remembered that if she hadn't invited Corinne to her party, she would have lost both a good friend and her dog.

# My Dumb Old Pussycat

## A TRUE STORY
### by Esther L. Vogt

Cricket came to live with me in 1973, a cuddly, tan-and-black, half-Siamese, half-alley cat. Because she liked to chase crickets, the name stuck. I enjoyed her company, for I lived alone.

Although she looked Siamese, Cricket had the happy-go-lucky personality of a plain old house cat. She didn't cry like her Siamese relatives. Though when she was upset (which wasn't often) she would wail and moan.

Cricket scampered, played, gobbled cat food, chased paper wads, and rolled miniature marshmallows on the kitchen floor like a very ordinary cat. I was glad she was well behaved. Sometimes I called her my "dumb old pussycat" because she was so very ordinary—for a Siamese.

In July 1983, I began to notice strange things around my house. Cricket's dish was always empty. I couldn't seem to keep it filled.

"What's gotten into you?" I scolded one day. "You've never packed away so much chow in all your nine lives!"

That wasn't all. Half-ripened tomatoes on the cabinet

were disturbed. Were Cricket's tastes changing? I also found small "messes" all over the house—on the windowsill, on the cabinet, in dark corners. And I poked an accusing finger at Cricket's black face.

"What's the matter? Can't you get to your litter box on time anymore?"

Cricket just looked at me with her soulful blue eyes and blinked.

Several nights strange thumps awoke me, and I heard tiny feet pattering on the kitchen floor. "That stupid cat!" I fumed. "One of these days I'll have enough of her shenanigans. She's getting to be impossible!"

Planning to go to Oklahoma a few mornings later to visit my two granddaughters, I got up early to pack. As I went to the front closet for a suitcase, I noticed a strong odor drifting through the slightly open closet door.

I slid the door open farther and reached in among the TV trays, old rugs, and folding chairs for my suitcase. Suddenly I thought I saw something move in the shadows. No, I decided. I couldn't have seen anything. My eyes must be playing tricks.

But I looked again. And to my amazement two big eyes peered back at me from the stack of rugs and trays. A wide open mouth hissed when I stretched my hand toward it.

Some fool stray cat? I wanted to grab it and jerk it out but something stopped me. What if the cat was wild—or maybe rabid? I'd better not risk it.

Hurrying to the phone, I dialed the police. "There's a rather nasty stray cat holed up in my closet, and I'm afraid to get it out," I blurted.

"Hang on. I'll be right over," Police officer Jerry said promptly.

Five minutes later he punched the doorbell, and I pointed to the closet.

He plunged in with his flashlight. "Here it is!" he cried, hitting it on the head. "I'm glad you called. It's no cat. It's a baby possum. Now how do you suppose it got into your closet?"

A possum? Horrors! Puzzled, I shook my head. "I'm sure I don't know," I said.

"If you'll get me a bag, I'll carry it out," he told me.

I brought the bag and watched as he put the wild creature in it and carried it outdoors. I thanked Officer Jerry for his help and said good-bye, still puzzled about the possum.

Later, as I packed, I thought about how Cricket used to bring in little, troubled creatures. She sometimes brought injured birds to me when I worked in the garden. One Sunday afternoon after playing outdoors, she pawed at the front door, begging to come in. As I opened the door, she streaked through the living room and into the kitchen. She had a wad of gray in her mouth. Another bird? She

dropped it on the floor and stood back, her blue eyes pleading.

A tiny gray cottontail rabbit cowered on the floor. Cricket apparently wanted to bring it to me. Perhaps she sensed it was scared and needed help. Her look plainly said, "Here, this creature needs someone. You take care of it."

Gently, I lifted the little bunny with an old towel and checked it carefully. It was wriggly and very much alive. I carried it outside and laid it under the ash tree in the front yard. After a while it hopped away.

Now I thought of Cricket's "kindness" to the poor, scared bunny. Could she have found the baby possum and brought it indoors for me to take care of? When I opened the door at her scratching at night, I didn't always bother to check if she were carrying in some creature in distress. I realized she must have brought in the possum without my knowing about it.

That was the only explanation. Perhaps Cricket wasn't an ordinary "dumb cat" after all. Maybe she had wanted to be kind. And I had accused her of many things for which the possum was to blame!

I cuddled Cricket in my arms and buried my face in her warm fur. "I'm sorry I blamed you for something you didn't do, Cricket. I'm also sorry I called you 'dumb,' when you only wanted to be kind. You really are special, you know!"

And she purred softly as though agreeing with me.

# The "Talking" Fish

*A NATURE STORY*
*by John Leedy,* PH.D.

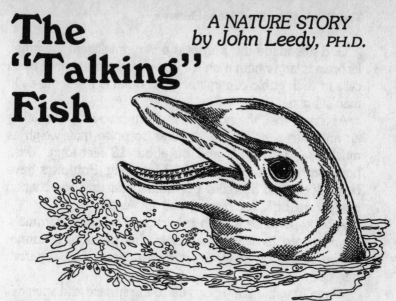

"Chirp, moan, whistle!" What strange sounds are coming over our underwater microphones! Strange to us, maybe, but not strange to porpoises. There's a whole school of them swimming around and "talking" over our hydrophones.

In porpoise language the chirp might mean "Come on, gang. Here comes the mullet. Let's eat." The moan could be "Oh, shucks, we missed." The whistle might be "We need help. Here comes a shark!"

The human ear can't pick up these high-pitched sounds. But marine biologists say that porpoises can hear fainter sounds and figure them out more accurately than any other animal.

Strangely, the porpoise has no vocal cords. Scientists aren't sure just how they make their high-pitched noises. But men have discovered that porpoises use this same noise-making equipment to find food, check water depth, and keep from bumping into objects.

God has made the porpoise a very intelligent mammal. Its brain is larger than man's. However, the number of brain cells in each cubic centimeter of its brain is the same as in man's brain.

As a mammal, the porpoise is warm-blooded. It breathes air and nurses its young. A large porpoise may weigh as much as 300 pounds and be about 12 feet long. Most, however, are between 6 and 12 feet long. Porpoises have been clocked at 30 miles per hour. Their torpedo-shaped bodies are built for high speed in water.

A baby porpoise is born tail first, unlike other mammals. Coming into its watery world in this position, it cannot drown. A quick twist by the mother releases the baby from her body.

When free, the baby pops up to the surface and snatches its first breath of air. Then it swims back down to its mother for its first meal. By using special muscles, the mother actually squirts milk into the baby's mouth.

Always nearby to help the mother and newborn porpoise is another female. She will help fight off sharks and be a nursemaid to the baby.

When attacked by sharks, the mother and nurse whistle for help. Then they charge the shark. Driving head-on at full speed, they strike the shark just behind its gills. As more and more porpoises come, they surround the shark and hammer at him until he's dead.

Porpoises are so expert at herding fish that they have been called "seagoing cowboys." The herding usually ends with the fish inside a circle of porpoises. With the fish corraled, the "cowboys" take turns charging into the school of fish and snapping up their dinner.

Like your favorite clown, this prankster is always grinning. His upturned mouth gives him a laughing face. But he is tough enough to kill sharks and clever enough to herd fish and loving enough to be a friend of man.

Because the porpoise is a mammal and breathes air, he has a single nostril on top of his head. This is really a blowhole. It is closed when the head is underwater. However, the nostril can be vibrated much like we vibrate our lips when we want to sound like a motorcycle. This is the porpoise "voice" we can hear.

Sounds of the porpoise have been taped and studied by Dr. Lilly at the Communication Research Institute at St. Thomas in the Virgin Islands. He learned that at times porpoises would imitate in a high voice, words he had said to them.

One porpoise was scolding back at the doctor in a voice so much like his that Dr. Lilly's wife laughed. Then the laugh was on Mrs. Lilly for the porpoise chuckled right back at her.

Perhaps one day man will unlock one more of God's mysteries—the language of animals. How exciting it would be to understand the porpoise and talk back and forth with this clever mammal.

" I LIKE HAVING A PEN PAL. "

# The Escape of Yellow Eyes

*A FICTION STORY by Betty Steele Everett*

As he crossed the yard to the shed he had built for Yellow Eyes, Tim heard Kim, his 12-year-old twin sister, come out onto the patio to watch him feed his pet red-tailed hawk.

*She likes Yellow Eyes,* Tim thought, *but she won't leave the house to see him perform. She can't believe that no one really notices her face.*

Kim had been a heroine in a fire the past spring. She had been baby-sitting and had saved two small children trapped upstairs. But Kim herself had been overcome by smoke and badly burned. Her left arm and face were both scarred.

All through the hot summer months, she had worn long-sleeved blouses to hide her arm. But there was no way to hide her face. Only once had she left the house since coming home from the hospital four months ago.

Even when school had started last month, she had begged to stay home. Tim brought her schoolwork home and Mother helped her.

*She's got to start going out,* Tim thought. *The longer she stays in, the harder it will be.*

But everything the family had tried so far had failed. Tim had gotten Kim to go out once after dark. But they had met some friends from school. Everyone had been embarrassed and had made Kim feel worse. She had not gone out again.

*Not even to church,* Tim thought as he put on the heavy glove he wore to protect his hand from the hawk's talons. *The doctor said we should encourage but not force her, but nothing seems to work.*

Now Tim took the bird from its cage and tossed it high into the air. Yellow Eyes rose slowly, and gracefully flew to the garage roof.

Tim raised his gloved fist in which he held a piece of meat. "Yellow Eyes, come!" he called.

The bird swooped down to rest on his hand and take the meat.

"Good Boy," Tim said, remembering the day Yellow Eyes had arrived. Kim was home from the hospital by then. She had watched Tim train Yellow Eyes, but had never helped.

Tim had started by taming or *manning* the hawk, as the book called it. He had put a hood over the bird's head, then carried him for hours on his gloved hand to get the hawk used to the perch. Yellow Eyes had weighed two pounds then. Now he was almost full-grown.

Tim had taught his pet to eat from his hand. Unless the bird knew there would be food in Tim's hand, he wouldn't come when called. Tim had used a long leash to get the hawk to fly to him, starting with short distances, then longer.

*Now after three months, he comes no matter how high he's flown,* thought Tim with pride.

Once news of a trained hawk got around, Tim and

Yellow Eyes were asked to appear at several athletic events and a store opening. They were a big hit.

Now Tim looked over at Kim. "How about that?"

"He's beautiful!" she called. "He glides so easily."

Tim tethered the bird to his perch on the lawn and went to join his sister. He had an idea.

"I'd like you to come with Yellow Eyes and me to the county children's home next week," he said as he sat down beside her. "I could use some help."

"I can't, Tim. I know what you think, but I just can't face people—even little kids. Next year, after the plastic surgery—"

"Kim, no one cares about those scars but you. The kids at school and church all know how you got them, and they know you. Sure, maybe the first couple of times will be hard, but the home is a good place to start. The kids will all be looking at Yellow Eyes. They won't pay any attention to you."

"The adults would. They'd stare, then look away, then try to think of something to say to show they hadn't noticed," Kim replied. "I know how it would be. Even our friends don't call on the phone anymore. And they don't have to look at me when they phone!"

"They might call if you'd stop shutting yourself up like a hermit!" Tim declared. Instantly, he was sorry for his sharp tone. But Kim *was* getting worse.

"You don't understand! You're still perfect!" she cried.

Tim sighed. What could he say? Yet he was sure she should be going back to school and taking part in her old activities.

When he came home from school on Thursday afternoon, Tim gave Kim her assignments, then went outside to feed Yellow Eyes. Kim followed as far as the patio.

The hawk was sitting on his perch, waiting. Tim slipped on the glove, then released him. Yellow Eyes rose high into the air.

"Hey!" Tim cried, watching the bird. "You're going too far! Come, Yellow Eyes! Come!" He held up his fist with the piece of meat, but the bird did not come. He flew higher.

"Yellow Eyes! Come!" Tim shouted. "Come!"

But the dark bird did not come swooping down from the sky. In fact, Tim could not even see the hawk now.

"Why won't he come?" Kim called. "He's always come before. What's wrong with him?"

"He's flown away!" Tim cried. He raised his arm again. "Yellow Eyes, come!" he shouted.

"He can't hear you anymore," Kim said. "O Tim, I'm sorry." Her eyes had filled with tears, Tim noticed as he came back to the patio where she stood. "He's escaped and he'll be killed."

Tim took a deep breath. "Don't cry, Kim. When I bought him, they said it was hard to keep a wild bird sometimes. They're not like cats and dogs. They don't love you—just the food you give them."

"Maybe he'll come back when he gets hungry," Kim said suddenly.

Tim brightened. "He's never been taught to hunt for himself as he would have been if he'd been raised in the wild. Maybe he won't be able to take care of himself and he'll come back. I'll call every 15 minutes or so."

For the rest of the afternoon, Tim went to the yard every quarter hour, raised his gloved fist, and called Yellow Eyes. But by dark the hawk had not returned.

"I'm sorry, Tim," Kim said when Tim finally agreed it was too dark to call anymore. "I liked Yellow Eyes too. He was a little like me, I thought. Taken away from the life he should have had, I mean. I know how much he meant to you—all the time you spent training him. But you said yourself he wouldn't be able to hunt food. Maybe he'll come back."

That night Tim slept badly. He kept dreaming of his hawk alone somewhere, without food.

He was up early the next morning. He hurried into his clothes and went outside. No sign of the hawk. Tim put on the glove as usual and held out a piece of meat. He called "Yellow Eyes! Come!" But the hawk didn't appear.

Just before he left for school, Tim tried again. Still no bird came swooping in from the sky or trees.

"I'll watch for him today," Kim promised. "I could hardly sleep last night, wondering about him."

School dragged for Tim. When the last bell finally rang, he rushed home. He was running up the walk when the front door burst open and Kim ran to meet him. "Yellow Eyes is back! He came to his perch about an hour ago—just as though nothing had happened! I've been watching him, talking to him from the patio. I was so afraid he'd fly away again."

Tim grinned, relieved. "Not when he's hungry. And he's probably starved by now. I'll feed him right away."

"You were right," Kim said as he put on his glove. "He came back when he realized he couldn't make it on his own." She sounded a little sad, Tim thought.

"I'll check his crop to be sure he's hungry," Tim said. He felt the bird's crop. Then he felt it again. "Kim, it's full. He must have hunted last night. He was never taught to hunt; it must be instinct."

"But if he could feed himself, why did he come back?" Kim asked as she came closer to look at Yellows Eyes.

Tim frowned. "I don't know. Maybe because he knows this is a safe place where he can get food if he needs it."

"Will he stay now?" Kim asked.

Tim shook his head. "Who knows? But I'll have to give him a chance to go if he wants to. I'll leave him untied and feed him, but he'll be free to leave if he wants and come back if he wants."

"But someday he won't come back," Kim said. "You'll lose him."

"I guess everything has to leave sometime. It'll be best for him—he can get used to his world slowly, then stay when he's ready."

"I guess you're right." Something in her tone made Tim glance sharply at her. She was staring at Yellow Eyes with a thoughtful look.

"I said before that I'm like you," she told the hawk quietly, "and I am. I've got to get back into my own world again too. I want to stay here where it's safe, but that's not the best thing. You knew it, didn't you, Yellow Eyes? And now I know it."

Tim grinned. "And you'll both make it, Sis."

Kim swallowed. "I wonder if Yellow Eyes was as scared as I am? But even if he was, he did it—and I guess that's what I have to do too. Tim, I'll go with you to the county home. I've got to start somewhere. With you and Mom and Dad and the Lord backing me up, I'll make it."

# When You Face a Lion

*A TRUE STORY*
*by Hal Olsen*

A FLOCK of egrets, white against the gray slopes of distant hills, flapped up into the sky. A band of rust-colored impala antelope bounded in panic across the plains. A family of warthogs raced away through the grass, their tails raised in warning of danger on the African plains.

*Something's got everything running scared,* Dr. Kenneth Allan said to himself.

The missionary doctor stopped, pulled his sun hat over his eyes, and looked over the sea of grass ahead. He saw nothing out of the ordinary—just mile on endless mile of sunburnt grass, dotted with flattopped thorn trees. It was a typical East African scene.

The nine African carriers walking ahead on the trail had not stopped. They trudged along under their loads without missing a step or looking from side to side. They didn't seem concerned over the flight of animal life. Maybe the animals had run because of man's intrusion.

Dr. Allan hesitated to judge anything by the conduct of

the nine men he had on this safari. In all his years of preaching trips through the territory of Kenya's Kamba tribe, he could not remember having a band of such lazy, slow-thinking workers.

*They'd be of little help in an emergency,* Dr. Allan thought, shaking his head.

He looked at his watch. It would soon be time for a welcome rest and a cup of tea, sweetened with condensed milk. Then they'd tramp for another two hours until they reached the next village. There, he and his helpers would hold a Gospel meeting, give medicine to the sick, and camp for the night.

The doctor leaned forward under the weight of the pack on his back—and almost ran into the man ahead of him. The carrier had stopped as had all those in front. The doctor could just barely see over the loads on the carriers' heads.

Jason, the leader of the single file of men, had raised his hand in silent signal. Slowly each man put his bundle on the ground. Dr. Allan did the same. All eyes were on Jason. Something was ahead in the grass and only Jason could see it.

Jason signaled again, making a fan-out motion with his arms. Each man seemed to know what to do. At once, four men went to the left of the leader and four went to his right. Each man walked briskly through the knee-high grass.

Jason made a grasping signal with his hands and all the men clasped hands to form a nine-man chain.

Dr. Allan was the last man in the single file safari and didn't understand what was going on. But as the human chain fanned out across the trail and into the grass, he followed close behind. He knew this was no game. There must be danger ahead.

Actually, so far, no one but the leader had seen what lay ahead until the chain of men went a few steps farther. Then everyone could see: Just a few yards in front of them lay a huge lioness with two young cubs at her side.

She lay on her stomach with her powerful paws pointing forward, her head held high. Her face was handsome and fierce. She stared intently at the men coming toward her.

Now the doctor realized what had happened: Jason had come upon the lioness without warning. There had been no time to run. And the old Kamba tribe instruction for a lone person coming upon a lion—standing completely still—would not have worked either. She had two cubs with her. She would be in no mood to show mercy.

One swipe of her forepaw could bring instant death to a man. To run or stand still would mean almost certain death. The lioness could maul the whole party in minutes. The plan Jason was directing was their only hope.

The men's eyes were open much wider now that they saw the lioness and her cubs, but they knew what they were doing and never faltered. Slowly but surely, they walked forward toward the big beast and her cubs.

The cubs lazed unconcernedly, but their mother suddenly came to a half-springing position. Still, the human chain moved forward. Dr. Allan followed right behind the band of men, breathing a prayer for God's protection.

The lioness looked into the eyes of each man, starting at one end of the chain and slowly moving toward the other end. Not one man showed signs of breaking or weakening. Again, her penetrating eyes swept the chain of men. If the plan was going to work, it had to work now.

Suddenly, the lioness let out a subdued roar, stood up, and dashed away into the bush. Her cubs followed.

The chain of men stood silent for a moment with their

hands still clasped. Then they all groaned with relief and sat down. They mopped their foreheads and smiled, for they had won.

Dr. Allan sat down too, with a new admiration for the men. He realized how he had misjudged them. He bowed his head and thanked the Lord aloud for His protection and the courage of the Africans.

That night, during an evangelistic meeting in the village where they camped, Dr. Allan reported the incident. "The Kamba trick worked, but if even one man had faltered, the lioness would have been upon us all in a flash.

"She studied each man's face, looking for a weak link in the chain. But not a man showed fear. In complete unity, the men faced the enemy and the lioness was overcome."

Dr. Allan never forgot that experience. He used the story to illustrate the truth of God's Word: "Resist the devil, and he will flee from you" (James 4:7, KJV).

"If godly men will stand in unity, without fear, they will overcome evil with good!" he would say with feeling. "And they will go forward in the strength of the assurance, 'greater is He that is in you, than he that is in the world' " (1 John 4:4, KJV).

# Run with the Lightning

*A FICTION STORY*
*by Jean Thompson*

Lightning flickered outside the kitchen window, dancing among the clouds above the mountains. A threatening mutter of thunder followed closely behind.

Megan sighed and put her milk glass in the sink. It was going to storm, and 12 was much too old to be afraid. Thunder and lightning were only natural forces, and wouldn't hurt her at all.

She said it firmly, as she had so many times, but every nerve was still stretched tight. She was getting along better than she used to. She no longer huddled with Pansy, both of them shaking in terror.

She smiled as she looked at Pansy who looked back out of sad spaniel eyes.

*Come on, Megan,* she said to herself. *You're stalling. You know you should go.*

Today was Wednesday, and she should have ridden to Marstons' on the school bus to feed their pets and water their plants. The Marstons had left on a trip early Tuesday morning. They had said she needn't go over Tuesday night, as they would leave plenty of food and water, but she must be sure to go Wednesday after school.

Megan had been daydreaming on the bus. She hadn't even realized they were at her stop until Kathy Lewis punched her in the ribs. Then Megan had stumbled off in a flurry of embarrassment, hearing the other kids giggling. Someone said sarcastically, "You'd think she'd know her own stop by now. She's been getting off here for a month."

It wasn't a month. It was only two weeks, but it seemed like a year.

It had sounded so terrific when her parents decided to sell the store and move to Colorado. Megan and Taffy, her best friend since kindergarten, had talked about it excitedly together. Of course they would miss each other, but they would write every day and they would visit each other in the summers. It would be so much fun to live on a ranch in Colorado, just like on TV. When Taffy came to see her, they would ride horseback together over the beautiful green hills.

But it wasn't like that at all. Instead of the glamorous ranch Megan had imagined, they lived in an ordinary house on just a few acres of land. There were no horses, and, with her older brother in college, it would be awhile before they could afford one. Both her parents worked in town to make ends meet. Worst of all, Megan had no friends. No one in the new school seemed to notice her.

Well, her parents wouldn't expect her to walk to Marstons'. It was three-quarters of a mile away and bad weather, besides. They could drive her there when they got home.

Megan went to her room and began writing a letter to Taffy.

Thunder rumbled again, like someone dragging something heavy on the other side of the hill. The trees in the yard shifted their branches restlessly as the wind began to blow.

Megan didn't know why she'd agreed to feed the Marstons' silly fat dog and ugly Siamese cat. She didn't like dachshunds, anyway—with their long sausagelike bodies and almost useless little legs. This one was even uglier than most. He sagged in the middle till his stomach practically dragged on the ground. He was really a gross little creature.

Pansy came into the bedroom and flopped at her feet. Thunder crashed, and Megan nearly leaped out of her chair. Pansy's feet scrabbled on the floor as she shot under the desk. A high, wailing howl came from the northeast corner of the house. Once Megan had read a story about the wind demon—and now she knew what it meant.

Then she remembered something else—her parents would be late tonight. There was an appointment with a lawyer about the sale of their store. They probably wouldn't be home until after 6:30.

Megan knew they would be tired and wouldn't want to drive her to Marstons'. She could imagine all the things they would say. She had heard them so often lately—all those words about accepting responsibilities and applying herself to the job at hand.

Surely they couldn't expect her to walk all that distance. They knew how she felt about storms. But if she hadn't been daydreaming, she could have ridden the bus. She had to admit it was her fault. How could she forget so many things in one day?

The window lit up with a brilliant flash, and thunder crashed again. The house actually shook, as if a load of bricks had been dropped on the roof. Pansy howled, and

Megan crouched under the desk to stroke her.

Maybe the Marstons' ugly dog, Snuffy, was just as afraid of storms as she was. He was all alone in the house except for the cat—who probably wasn't much comfort. Maybe Snuffy was crouched under something, crying in terror. And he was probably hungry and thirsty. It was bad enough to be alone and frightened without being hungry besides.

Megan stood up. She had decided she would walk over to the Marston's. She would accept her responsibilities and show her parents she was growing up. It was really childish to be afraid of a little wind and noise.

She put on her windbreaker, got Pansy's leash, and snapped it on. "Come on, Pansy. Keep me company."

The dog braced her feet and pulled back. Megan pulled harder and Pansy whined pitifully.

"Come on, Pansy. Don't be such a coward." She dragged the dog out and bent over to reassure her. As soon as the tension slackened on the leash, the dog shot back under the desk.

"You cream puff!" Megan yelled at her. "That's what you are—a sissy dog. Just stay home and whine. I'll go without you."

Megan slammed out of the house and raced down the road. The wind drove at her, flattening her jacket against her body, whipping her hair out from under her hood. Half the sky flashed into sudden radiance, and Megan hunched her shoulders, waiting for the crash. It came, shaking the world around her.

Megan's knees felt weak and trembly. Maybe she should go back. If she went on, she might get struck by lightning. Someone would find her later, lying dead beside the road.

She turned around. A car was coming behind her. Maybe they would give her a ride! (But she wasn't supposed to ride with strangers.) If they offered her a lift, what should she do? Which was worse—to walk in the storm or risk riding with someone she didn't know?

She turned again and walked on, listening to the sound of the wheels on the gravel behind her. The car was going very slowly. They were going to stop. What should she say?

But the car passed by. Megan had a glimpse of two old ladies, faces set, eyes straight ahead.

*They might at least have looked at me,* she thought.

Rain came down in a sudden rush, drenching her until she was almost blinded. She started to run again and ran until her chest ached and she thought it would split.

The Marstons' house was in view now. She felt pounds lighter—almost floating with exhilaration. She'd made it—and it hadn't been all that bad. She felt so good she actually began to look forward to seeing Snuffy and the Siamese cat.

The Marstons had given her a key to the side door.

"Snuffy," she called. "Mandarin. Here, kitty. Come, Snuffy."

Only silence greeted her, so she went to the kitchen. Two bowls were sitting on newspapers—huge bowls, still half full of dried food. The water bowls were almost full too, and there was even canned food. It was crusty and unappetizing, but there was plenty of it—enough to feed a whole army of dogs and cats. They hadn't needed her at all.

Megan plodded through the house, watering the plants. She heard a low growl when she went into the living room. Snuffy was under one of the tables in a corner.

"Snuffy! There you are! Don't be afraid. I'm a friend." She held out her hand, but the dog snarled again.

"Oh, you miserable beast. I don't know why I came at all. It was just a big fat waste of time."

She didn't see Mandarin. He was probably hiding some-place too.

She glanced out of the window and noticed a sudden flurry of movement across the field. She saw it again—something tossing up and down. She strained her eyes to see through the rain. It was a horse's head, reaching above the grass; then it dropped down—and up again.

She didn't know much about horses, but it was obvious he was in trouble. She trotted out through the rain to see him better.

The horse was a young palomino belonging to Kathy Lewis, the girl who had told her it was time to get off the bus. Megan had heard Kathy talking about him at school. She was so proud of having a registered palomino of her very own.

He was lying on his side. Both rear legs and one front leg were tangled in the wire fence. He was trying to get up—

**79**

lunged as far as he could, and then fell back.

"Oh, don't do that," Megan cried. "You'll cut yourself. Lie still."

She stroked his head and he rolled his eyes at her. The fence wasn't barbed and he wasn't bleeding yet; but if he kept thrashing around, he would hurt himself.

He started up again and Megan pressed his head down. "Oh, please. Lie still."

The horse made a strangled sound—half whinny, half cry—and tried to jerk away from her. She held on desperately, forcing him to stay down. With one hand, she tried to slip the wire off his front leg, but it was too tight. It would take wire cutters to release him.

She ran back to the house and picked up the phone. It was dead! Frantically, she jiggled the hook up and down. Nothing happened.

It was nearly two miles to the Lewis house, but the road made a long loop around a steep stony ridge. If she cut over the top, it would make the distance less than half as long.

Megan hardly felt the rain as she ran across the pasture. Three cows, standing under the scant shelter of some cottonwood trees, looked at her as she pounded by. Yesterday she would have been afraid of them, but today there wasn't time to worry.

Megan scrambled over the fence and started up the hill. She thought about rattlesnakes. She had heard they were out there among the white sage and the low cacti and the rocks, but she switched her mind away. There was no point in thinking about snakes now.

The hill was steep and she paused to rest. She hadn't gone as far as she thought. The house and field still looked disappointingly close. She couldn't see the horse. There were trees around the corner where he was caught, and the rain was like a veil between her and the horse.

She turned and plodded on. The trail was too steep for her to hurry. It was all she could do to keep moving one foot in front of the other. She rested again, and this time the house seemed quite far below.

The wind was stronger up here. It beat into her face, driving the rain into her eyes. She scrambled over an outcropping of stones. Her foot jarred a rock loose and it rattled down the hill behind her. Then she slipped and fell. She was sure her knee was bleeding, but she didn't have time to look. She jumped up and plodded on.

She was in brush now, and it was impossible to tell how far she was from the top. She flailed her way through—the branches scratching her face and hands. Suddenly she was out in the open. The crest was just a few yards away. Each leg seemed to weigh about a thousand pounds, but she picked them up and put them down—and then she was on the top.

She collapsed on the ground, panting. Before she was really ready to move, she got up and started down the other side. Going down was almost as hard as it had been to go up. Her knees felt weak and rubbery and threatened to buckle at every step. At least she could go a little faster and she scrambled down the steep ridge, jumping and sliding.

Finally she was at the Lewis house, pounding on the door. Kathy herself opened it, looking startled and apprehensive. She stared at Megan as though she had never seen her before.

*She probably never has seen me before,* thought Megan. *I don't think she's ever really looked at me.*

"Kathy," she gasped. "I'm Megan—the new girl. I just

found your horse. He's caught in the fence by the Marstons' house.

Kathy ran into the kitchen. "Dad, come quick. Sundance is in trouble."

"You're quite a girl, Megan," Mr. Lewis said later. "You saved a valuable horse."

"Sundance is special," said Kathy. "I couldn't stand it if anything happened to him."

"You didn't do bad for a city girl who's afraid of thunder, lightning, and cows," said Megan's father, smiling at her.

They were all sitting in Megan's living room, drinking hot chocolate. Megan was barefoot and in her bathrobe, drying out. It was a little embarrassing to have everyone fussing over her, although she was glad Sundance hadn't been seriously hurt.

"Someday I hope I can have a horse like Sundance," she said.

"I hope so too," said Kathy. "Then we can ride together. Why don't you come over this weekend and I can start teaching you to ride? Then you'll be ready when you do get your horse."

"I'd love to," said Megan. "Can I, Dad?"

"Oh, I think it can be arranged."

The Lewises got up to go. "I'll see you tomorrow, Megan," Kathy said. "I'll save you a seat on the bus."

After they had gone, Megan hugged her knees and thought, *Going to the Marstons' was worthwhile after all.*

For the first time since coming to Colorado, she actually looked forward to going to school. She knew tomorrow was going to be a good day.

# Wild Horse of Africa

## by Gloria A. Truitt

I am a grazing animal
  Of Africa's wild plains.
Unlike my relative, the horse,
  I can't be led with reins.

Although I'm quite attractive in
  My stripes of black and white,
Never get too close to me
  For I will kick and bite.

Like other mother zebras, I
  Give birth to just one foal,
And when it's dusk you'll find us at
  Our favorite water hole.

© 1986 Gloria Truitt

# Bacon for Breakfast

*A FICTION STORY*
*by Mary Marks Cezus*

"And we thank You for this food. Amen," Father prayed.

"No thank you for this food," Brian said.

David looked up at his two-year-old brother Brian and watched as he pushed his bowl of oatmeal away and crossed his chubby arms angrily.

"Brian, what's wrong with your oatmeal?" Mother asked as she pushed the bowl toward Brian again.

"I don't like oatmeal. It's yucky! I like bacon."

David had heard this conversation often lately. Now that Mom's job was gone and Dad was working four days instead of five, many things had changed. If David hadn't been so busy thinking about Whiskers, some of those changes probably would have bothered him more.

David wasn't crazy about oatmeal either, but he wanted to be on his way as soon as possible, so he ate his breakfast quickly. One more week and Whiskers would live here instead of at the pet store!

Today Brian was not ready to be coaxed into eating his

cereal. He picked up the bowl and dumped it on the floor. When Mom scolded him, Brian began to cry. It was then that David looked up to see his father's face. It looked the way David felt when he was hollered at for something he didn't know was wrong. His face looked angry, sad, and hurt all at the same time.

"Don't scold him, Lucy. He's not old enough to understand."

David finished eating and gathered his things for school. Brian was still sobbing quietly, while his parents sat at the table without talking. David didn't like the quiet. He wished the dress shop would open again. He wished the mill would have more work for his father. He wished it were next Wednesday. Next Wednesday he would be 10. Next Wednesday he would own Whiskers.

When David reached the pet shop, Whiskers gave him his special greeting. Mr. Barker said he could always tell when David was outside by the way Whiskers barked. He said that Whiskers and David belonged together like apple pie and ice cream.

When David asked him if someone else might buy Whiskers before his birthday came, Mr. Barker had said, "I don't think so, Dave. Puppies aren't selling as quickly as they did a while back. You might want to make friends with the other fox terrier just in case, though."

So this morning David said hello to both Whiskers and Charlie. They barked and jumped against the window. The paper displaying the fox terrier's price looked large and bold this morning. As David looked at it, he remembered his father's face. He didn't stay long at the pet shop. The bright numbers seemed to jump out at him.

At lunch, Scott West talked excitedly about a fox terrier he was hoping to buy. Scott seemed to own every new toy that came along. As he described the dog's bright eyes and mottled, wirehaired coat, David felt sure he was talking about Whiskers.

"When I talked to Mr. Barker, he said I have to wait until next week to buy Bugsby because some other kid thinks his dad might buy him the dog for his birthday."

David wondered if Scott remembered he had a birthday next week. He didn't really care about all the things Scott owned, but Scott knew how to make it hurt when he had something somebody else wanted. David was glad he hadn't told anyone about Whiskers.

When David stopped to see Whiskers on his way home, the first thing that caught his eye was the price tag, and that made him think of his father's face and Brian's tears. He hardly noticed Whisker's sparkling eyes or wagging tail. He hurried home. It wasn't much fun playing with Whiskers through the glass with that price tag glaring at him.

Dinner tasted plain. David found it hard to swallow. Noticing that Brian didn't eat very much, he wondered when they had last had a special treat. He hadn't noticed because his mind had been with Whiskers.

As he prepared for bed, David realized he needed to have a talk with God. It was easier to talk to God than to most people.

"Dear Heavenly Father," he began, "I've got a problem and I don't know what to do. I really want this dog. I've named him Whiskers and I know he'd be lots of fun. But he would cost quite a bit of money. We don't have much right now. I had it all figured out until lunchtime. Then Scott said he wanted to buy Whiskers, only he called him Bugsby.

"I know this is mean, but I don't want Scott to have Whiskers. You see, I still think of him as my dog."

David was crying now. He was glad it was dark and he

was alone. He didn't feel almost 10.

"If only Scott didn't rub it in when he got something someone else wanted, I wouldn't mind so much. I know he will show off all the tricks he teaches Whiskers, I mean Bugsby, and then say something like, 'Don't you wish you had a dog like this, David?' I just know he will.

"My parents would buy Whiskers for me. I heard Dad say to Mom the other day (they didn't know I could hear them), 'I promised him. We'll find a way.'

"Today, I thought about how much Whiskers would cost. We'd have to buy dog food and take him to the vet. Dad said we'd need a fence around the yard too. I know that would cost a lot.

"If Whiskers were mine, I'd teach him to play dead and speak and fetch. I'll bet I could teach him things nobody taught a dog before. He looks so smart! What should I do, God? I want Whiskers so much it hurts. It really does."

Then there were no more words, only silent tears sliding slowly down his cheeks. He thought about how God had sacrificed His only Son for the whole world, including David. He knew that was God's answer.

"I'll ask Mom and Dad if they'll buy me some clothes instead of a dog. I really need shoes. And I'll ask them if we can have bacon for breakfast as a birthday treat. Brian will like that. Maybe Scott will let me teach Bugsby some tricks, Lord. I knew You would help. Thanks a lot."

# Noisiest Arctic Animal

*by Gloria A. Truitt*

I live along the Arctic shores
  And make the loudest sounds.
My hairless skin looks much too loose
  For my three thousand pounds!

Down in the ocean depths I dive,
  Sometimes three hundred feet,
And there my ivory tusks scoop up
  The shellfish that I eat.

All day long I dine on fish...
  A hundred pounds, at least...
For any walrus like myself,
  This is an *average* feast!

© 1986 Gloria Truitt

# A Masked Bandit

*A TRUE STORY*
*by Jane C. Foss*

Mike opened the back door of the downstairs utility room and looked into a furry, masked face. Two shiny black eyes stared back at him—two frightened black eyes.

"Beth, come quick!" he called to his older sister. "There's a raccoon at our back door."

Beth put down her book and looked over Mike's shoulder. "That's a raccoon all right. What's he doing with the storage cabinet?" The animal was standing with his front paw resting on the cabinet just outside the door.

"He's trying to get something to eat," said Mike.

"Sorry, fella," replied Beth. "I don't think you can get in. Dad fixed the catch after you and your pals broke in last week. But don't worry; we'll get you something." She turned to her brother. "Get some dog food from the bucket and put it out on the step. He'll like that just as much as the birdseed from the cabinet."

Mike scooped up some dry dog food and cautiously opened the screen door. He poured the food on the step

near the raccoon. The animal didn't move except to droop a little. His left foot remained on the cabinet latch.

"Look, Beth. His paw is bleeding." Mike pointed to the foot the animal seemed to be leaning on. Beth moved closer to the door.

"I think he's stuck. His paw is stuck in the slot," she said.

The storage cabinet was really an old soft drink machine that the children's older brother had had in his room. When Dan went off to college, it had been placed outside and

**90**

used to store birdseed and grain for the many varieties of wildlife that came daily—or nightly—for dinner in the family's backyard. The coin slot no longer worked, but the raccoon had apparently tried to get into the cabinet and had gotten his claws stuck in the slot.

"We gotta get him loose. He's hurt. He may have been there all night. See how tired and scared he looks. What'll we do?" Mike asked.

"First of all, we'll stay calm and not scare him anymore. Hand me the broom, please. I'll see if I can nudge him loose with the handle." Beth slowly held the broom out toward the stuck paw. The frightened animal hissed and pushed the broom away with his free paw.

"What else can we try? We gotta help him." Mike was close to tears. "How about calling the fire department? I read a story in school about a fireman saving a cat."

"Good idea. But the raccoon isn't up high so we really don't need a ladder. Let's call the police department instead. They may have someone who can help."

Mike watched the trapped animal while Beth went upstairs to phone. The black eyes looking back at him held pain as well as fear. The furry body sagged against the cabinet. Mike made soothing sounds to comfort the animal. "We'll get you loose. Don't worry, fella. Just a few minutes longer."

In a very short time the doorbell rang and a police officer joined the children.

"I heard your call on my car radio. I was only a block away so I came right over." The policeman looked out at the raccoon. "Well, you've gotten yourself into a pickle, haven't you?" The animal looked back at the policeman with fear and perhaps pleading in his masked eyes.

"I tried to get him loose with the broom handle, but I just

**91**

scared him," Beth said. "I was so afraid I'd hurt him that my hands were shaking."

"I've had some experience with wild animals," the policeman said. "Let me have that broom."

The policeman opened the door and moved toward the raccoon, talking gently to the animal. "Just relax, Buddy; I'll have you loose in a minute." He skillfully pushed the slot with the broom handle, and the paw was loose. Instantly the raccoon was on all four legs, scrambling up the steps and off into the woods at the back of the yard.

"Will he be OK?" Mike asked anxiously. 'His foot was bleeding."

"He may have chewed it a little trying to get free. But he sure took off in a hurry. He'll be just fine in a day or so, probably be back to help himself to your dog food."

"Thanks so much, Officer. It's good to know you can come so quickly when we need help." Beth shook the policeman's hand.

"I didn't know the police took care of raccoons," Mike said.

"Well, we don't get many raccoon calls, but we always try to help any way we can," the officer said. "Remember that, young fellow. When you need help, give us a call."

"I'm going to put some tape over that slot so no one else will get caught," said Mike when the policeman had gone.

"Good thinking," replied his sister. "And let's put out some birdseed and more dog food in case our friend comes back tonight."

# Raccoons on the Prowl

## A NATURE STORY
### by Alta Elizabeth Snyder

Late one summer evening, our family decided to camp out in our own yard after a late picnic supper. Suddenly we heard a shrill, "Oo-loo-loo-loo!"

Our whole family jumped. What was it?

Then, only a few yards from us, we saw a mother raccoon and four furry babies shuffle into our big cornfield. They were after our corn!

We watched as Mother Raccoon reached up and pulled down ears of corn, stripped off the husks, and then shared them with her young. As they ate, the raccoon family whistled to each other in that same quivery, shrill "Oo-loo-loo-loo."

We found out later that raccoons like other food too, and will help themselves to them in the same bold way.

Some of their favorites are sweet corn and fruit. They will climb wild grapevines and eat the sour fruit for hours. They also eat papaw berries, blackberries, wild cherries, pears, apples, acorns, and other nuts. Or, in meadows, they snap up grasshoppers, crickets, and katydids—in fact, anything small that moves. Raccoons have a good appetite and eat greedily.

Sometimes the raccoon is described as a bandit, perhaps partly because of the way he helps himself to other people's property, but also because of the dark "mask" he wears over his eyes. And, if you make close friends with a raccoon, he may prove he is a thief by picking your pockets!

Now, if you were to look only at Mr. Raccoon's "hands," you would think he was a gentleman instead of a thief. His two front paws have four long black fingers peeping out of gray fur mitts. His hind feet have five toes and a heel. But all his paws are covered with a soft, smooth black "kid" covering, much like fancy gloves.

Of course, we must be fair to Mr. Raccoon. He steals but doesn't know better. He is only following his animal instinct to satisfy his big appetite and curiosity when he helps himself to things that don't belong to him.

He is also a good fisherman. He waddles along a stream, sniffing and snuffing as he peers into a moon-silvered brook. When he sees something edible, a polliwog, a green frog, a minnow, a water beetle, a worm, or a small snake— he quickly grabs it with his fingers.

But before eating, he washes his catch to remove sand or mud. The raccoon is a very clean animal. Part of his Latin name means "the washer." If you have a pet coon, he will appreciate a pan of water in which to dunk his food and wash his hands and feet after eating.

The raccoon's popular name was given to him by Indians. It means "he who scratches with his hands." His long claws are perfect for digging. And he can climb and hang from trees like a trapeze artist. He fools hunters and dogs by climbing a tree and peeking out of the leaves at them. If the hunter tries to shake him out, he may make a long jump or swing his heavy body to another tree in an effort to get away in the dark.

Coons live in families, usually in a den tree. Sometimes they have other "hunting lodges" if food is scarce. They usually live at the woodland edges, near a brook, pond, or marsh. However, they have been known to make themselves at home in the city in backyards, attics, and sewers.

The young are taught by their parents to hide their trails. They will cross a brook two or three times before settling down to hunt. They even run up and down various trees to confuse anything that may follow them.

Sometimes they like to be alone. Up in a tree crotch, curled up and looking like a Davy Crockett cap, a contented coon may twitter a pretty song, chirping like a bird.

All in all, the coon is one of God's more lively and lovable creatures. And He lives just as His Creator intended him to.

"YOU COULD HAVE A BREAKFAST LIKE THAT TOO IF YOU'D FIX IT YOURSELF LIKE HE DOES."

# False Alarm

*A FICTION STORY*
*by Victor E. Johnson*

Ten-year-old Billy Benson turned his horse toward Signal Hill. "C'mon, Flash," he urged. "It's not far. Get up!" He pressed his heels against the horse's sides and they were off with a speed that almost unseated the young rider. Dust rose behind them as they galloped.

The trail they followed took them past a grove of tall pine trees, fragrant in the autumn sun, then through a clear, rock-strewn brook. Beyond the stream, the trail narrowed to a path that zigzagged upward past trees and brush growing on the side of the steep, cone-shaped mountain called Signal Hill. According to legend, Indians had used the peak, before the white man's arrival, to send smoke signals to their people in the villages far out on the prairie.

Flash was breathing hard as they climbed Signal Hill, and Billy stopped him to rest. "Easy, old fellow. It's pretty steep here. Besides, I want to look for arrowheads. Hey, there's one now!" Swinging down from the saddle, he picked up a piece of flint, then flipped it away. "I was wrong. That stone was never used on an arrow. Guess I'll look near Council Oak. Aunt Nell's arrowhead came from there. She says Indians used to camp there years ago."

For an hour Billy searched. Then, hot and tired, he tied Flash's reins to a low branch of a gnarled oak. Taking a canteen of water and a sandwich from his saddlebags, he sat down in the shade to eat.

Overhead, a squirrel chattered. A blue jay flew close, screaming a loud "Thief! Thief!" It reminded Billy of the birds in the park at home, so tame they'd almost eat from your hand.

Billy's home was in Chicago. But things had happened which moved him to Montana.

Mother, suddenly ill, was taken to the hospital for a long series of tests. Fearing Billy would get into trouble in the city, Dad had arranged for him to spend a few months at the Donner ranch in southern Montana.

Mike and Nell Donner were Billy's favorite uncle and aunt. Living with them was fun—especially when Billy rode with Uncle Mike and Jack, the hired man, as they worked with the Donner herd of black Angus cattle.

There were times, though, when Billy wasn't happy. He would think of his mother, and questions would fill his mind. Why did she have to get sick? Why didn't God heal her? Billy had prayed for healing. Nothing happened. Did God really answer prayer? As Billy ate, his mind went over the familiar questions one more time. As usual, there were no answers. Just misery.

Flash's rhythmic chewing stopped. Wide-eyed, with ears pointed forward, he stared at a bush a short distance away. A black animal, nearly hidden by leaves, looked back at them. Billy's heart began to pound. He thought, *It's a bear!* Quickly he untied Flash, leaped into the saddle, and raced toward the ranch house where Uncle Mike and Jack were repairing a tractor.

Minutes later, Uncle Mike looked up as a sweaty horse and rider entered the machine shed. "What's the matter?" he asked with a grin. "You look as if you'd seen a ghost!"

Billy shook his head. He was panting. "I think—I saw—a bear!"

The grin faded. "A bear? How big?"

"Just a cub. But—I figured his mother was near. We left—real fast."

His uncle nodded. "A mother bear can be awfully mean. I'll get my gun while you walk Flash to cool him a bit. A horse that's lathered as heavily as he is must be treated carefully or he may get sick."

Jack, wiping grease from his hands, was heading toward the corral. "I'll get horses for the three of us, Mr. Donner." His usual cool speech remained unchanged by excitement. "Which one will you want, sir?"

"No horses, Jack. They're afraid of bears. Bring the Jeep."

Uncle Mike strode to the house. Soon he returned, carrying a heavy rifle. His revolver, in a holster at his side, hung from a wide belt ringed with gray-tipped cartridges. The Jeep pickup truck roared into the yard, and they clambered in.

Conversation ceased as they approached the huge oak where Billy had eaten his lunch. "There's the bush!" he whispered.

Jack stopped the Jeep and reached for his binoculars. Silently, carefully, he focused on the figure behind the bush. A slow grin spread across his face. "It's a calf," he said, chuckling. "Billy's 'bear' is just a little black calf!"

Billy's face reddened. "How could I tell?" he cried. "I

could only see part of him!"

Uncle Mike said sternly, "Hush, both of you!" They listened silently. From far away came the long, low "moo" of a cow calling her calf.

Uncle Mike reached for the rope that hung coiled behind the driver's seat. "Take this lariat, Jack," he said. "See if you can catch that calf. We'll take him to his mother in the next pasture. He got through the fence, somehow, and wandered over here. If he doesn't get milk soon, he'll starve."

As Jack sneaked toward the bush, the frightened calf leaped to his feet. Jack cast perfectly, dropping his rope's noose around the calf's neck, and dragged the struggling animal to the Jeep. Together they hoisted the little Angus into the truck. Jack, still holding the rope, jumped in beside him. "I'll hold him in," he said. "Let's go."

Near the spot where the cow stood, Uncle Mike stopped the Jeep and opened the gate. "OK, Jack," he called. "Bring the calf. Make sure the cow sees him, then let him go."

Jack carried the calf through the gate. He was stooping to loosen the rope when the cow snorted angrily and charged him. She hit him hard from behind and he fell sprawling.

Quick as a springing cat, Uncle Mike pounced for the calf and gave it a mighty shove. The calf ran, bawling. The cow followed a few steps, then turned again toward Jack. Uncle Mike's revolver boomed, firing shots in quick succession. The heavy bullets sprayed dust into the cow's face as they raked the ground. Dazed, the angry beast backed away, then ran after her calf.

Jack limped to the Jeep. Brushing dirt from his clothes, he climbed slowly in beside Billy.

"Are you hurt badly?" Billy asked.

Jack shook his head. "I'll be OK. Sorry I made fun of our little black calf. He and his mom were just as mean as a couple of real bears."

"Look," said Uncle Mike. "There's a good mother."

The cow had stopped and was licking her calf with her long, rough tongue. The calf was beginning to nurse, sucking milk from the cow's udder. Billy scrambled out of the Jeep to watch.

"Lucky you found him, Billy," said Uncle Mike. "He needed his dinner."

Billy asked, "Why was that cow so angry at us? We weren't hurting her calf; we were helping him."

Uncle Mike looked thoughtful. "She was too upset to know the difference," he said. "When she saw Jack close to her calf, she wanted him out of the way. A cow will fight 'most anything to save her baby."

"Sometimes," continued Uncle Mike, "people are as foolish as that poor cow. When things go wrong, we get so excited we fight everyone—even God. We need to slow down and think. Then we'll realize God is on our side. As the Bible says, 'All things work together for good to them that love God'" (Romans 8:28, KJV).

Billy looked up keenly into his uncle's calm, tanned face. "You really believe that, don't you?" he asked.

"Sure do," said Uncle Mike. "How about you?"

Billy nodded. He felt good inside. Somehow, things would be all right—even for his sick mother—for God controls all things.

# The Great Chicken Enterprise

*A FICTION STORY*
*by Lois Leader*

Perri Dayton sat on the floor, studying the contents of a small yellow booklet. All around her were scattered booklets and papers of various colors. The collection extended to the hallway, causing her brother Ronald to trip as he entered the room.

"Look at this mess!" he exclaimed.

"Be careful," Perri responded, "or you'll tear them."

"Oh, by all means, I mustn't tear them. It doesn't matter if I break my neck!" Ronald stooped and picked up one of the offending booklets. "*Raising Chickens for Fun and Profit*," he read aloud, looking questioningly at Perri. "What's all this?"

"I'm going into the chicken business!" Perri told him excitedly.

"But starting a business takes money!" Ronald exclaimed. "How much do you have?"

"The $10 I earned baby-sitting for Mrs. Sewell," she said.

Ronald rocked back on his heels and laughed. "Any day you can start a business with $10!"

Perri looked down at the bulletin entitled *Necessary Equipment for Poultry Keeping*. The list covered two columns. Perri's jaw took on a determined look. "I'm going to try."

That week she began to work on what her family called "Perri's Great Chicken Enterprise." Dad got a catalog from a local feed store and Perri proudly wrote out her order for 20 Barred Plymouth Rock pullets.

When her brother asked why in the world she wasn't ordering chickens, Perri told him, "Pullets are female chickens under a year old. When you order pullet chicks there's always some chance you may get a few roosters. Barred Rocks are a good egg and meat breed."

"Ha!" Ronald shouted. "That'll be the day when you cook a bird you raised from a chick. I've seen you carry beetles outside rather than stomp on them."

Perri didn't say anything; she knew Ronald was right and hoped there wouldn't be too many roosters.

The catalog also taught her that going into the chicken business wasn't cheap. "Dad, these prices are awful!" she cried in dismay.

Dad came to look over her shoulder. He pointed to the display of chicken feeders and waterers. "You can make these yourself with tin cans. For the chick brooder, you can use a box and a light bulb. Study over the catalog again, and I think you'll find many things you can make yourself."

Saturday morning, Perri went "treasure hunting" for her enterprise. The Daytons lived on the outskirts of town, surrounded by desert. Where the highway crossed their road, people often dumped their rubbish. Perri's father usually hauled this trash to the town dump with words about people's thoughtlessness in defacing God's creation. Perri disliked trash dumping as much as her father, but today she was glad Dad hadn't recently cleaned it up.

"Look what the cat's dragging in!" Ronald shouted as she dragged her day's find down the road. But he did run to help her untangle herself from the net of chicken wire.

"Where'd you find that?" he asked.

"Down at the bottom of the ravine where everyone dumps their stuff. There's an old cabinet down there too. It should make a great brooder!"

Ronald laughed, but there was a note of admiration in his voice when he said, "When you get something into your head, you sure stick to it."

The next week Perri was a busy 11-year-old. She hauled the cabinet home and made it into a chick brooder by hanging a light bulb from a hook at the top. From a collection of cans saved for her by Mom, she made a number of waterers and feeders. She dug post holes, buried posts, and strung chicken wire. The day before the chickens were due to arrive, Perri looked over the fruit of her labor with great satisfaction.

Saturday morning dawned cloudy and dark but the day couldn't have been brighter for Perri. Dad brought the chicks home! Perri sat in front of the brooder and watched joyfully as the tiny gray birds scurried back and forth between the waterers and feeders. The memory of all her hard work made the sight that much more beautiful.

Dad came out and knelt beside her. He seemed to know just what she was thinking, for he said, "One of the great gifts the Lord gives us is happiness in the work of our hands."

"That's true," Perri said. "If I'd been able to buy all that expensive stuff from the catalog, it wouldn't be half so neat."

Dad smiled then looked at his watch. "You'd better finish up here. We're going out to Aunt Hannah's, and I want to get there before the storm hits."

Perri rechecked the waterers and feeders and made sure the thermometer read 90 degrees, for the young chicks had to be kept warm.

Her mind was on the chicks most of the way to Aunt Hannah's. It wasn't until a loud clap of thunder startled her that Perri realized the storm was upon them. Rain drummed on the car. She had never seen so much rain fall at one time.

"There's Aunt Hannah's road," Dad called out. He sounded relieved.

As they pulled into her driveway, Aunt Hannah came running out into the rain. She led them into her front room, talking excitedly.

"I'm certainly glad to see all of you safe and sound! Did you know this is the worst storm we've had in 20 years? Why, people on the south side of town are having to leave their homes because of flooding, and in your area the power lines are down. You won't have any power until tomorrow morning, so you might as well spend the night here. . . . What's the matter?"

Perri had run out of the room and upstairs. Slamming the door of the spare bedroom behind her, she threw herself onto the window seat and stared out at the churning storm with angry eyes, then burst into tears. She didn't look up when she heard Dad enter the room.

"That's how I feel, Dad," Perri said flatly, nodding toward the violent scene outside.

"I know, Hon."

"The brooder will get cold, and the chicks will die."

"Yes." Dad was silent for a moment, then said, "Honey, the Lord doesn't promise us that things will never go wrong. But He *does* promise to be with us."

"But I worked so hard!" she cried.

"Yes, that makes it hurt all the more. But think of this, Perri. Many people will lose their homes and all they have worked for because of this flooding. We may have to take some of them into our home for a while. Perhaps, through your own loss, you'll be able to reach out to someone else and help them in a special way."

Dad put his arm around Perri's shoulder and gave her a hug. Without saying any more, he left the room.

Perri continued to stare out at the storm. Downstairs, she could hear the crackle of the radio as the announcer gave the latest news bulletins. Volunteers were being sought to take in families who had left their homes because of the flooding.

Perri still felt that dull, hollow ache when she thought about the chicks. But now she realized that others were feeling the same ache when they thought about their homes. And she knew the "great chicken enterprise" would have to wait.

# How Winter's Creatures Keep Warm

## A NATURE STORY
### by Olga Osing

Many creatures sleep during the cold winter months, but others stay wide awake. They are busy searching for food— but how do they keep warm?

Feathers always make a warm covering for their owners.

The woodpecker makes sure it gets all the warmth the feathers can give by fluffing them up. Sometimes during winter small woodpeckers look like fluffy balls.

Woodpeckers like to live in holes in trees during winter, as do other birds like nuthatches and chickadees. Pigeons and starlings in cities seek shelter on ledges of concrete buildings that have soaked up warmth during sunny days. On farms, sparrows and finches go into barns and haystacks.

Slate-colored juncos (ofter called snowbirds) roost in trees and sit close together to keep warm. Seeking warmth in flocks is also the habit of the small quail with reddish brown feathers known as bobwhites. When it is cold, bob-whites make a shallow dent in the snow. Then they form a circle with their tails in and heads out. By keeping their heads facing outward they can watch for any danger that may approach.

The ruffled grouse roost on tree branches. But often they jump into snowdrifts to keep warm, moving their bodies around to make a tiny igloo. God has given this species of grouse comblike structures which grow from the sides of their toes so they can stay on top of the snow.

The ptarmigan, an Arctic bird of the grouse family, also grows extra feathers that cover its feet and legs. Its plumage changes color according to the season. It is black, brown, and white in summer and pure white in winter.

Not only do some birds grow extra feathers for the cold months, but many four-footed creatures grow extra hair. Rabbits and hares grow springy hairs between their toes. These hairs grow so long that they are often an inch in length. In this way the little animals' paws avoid the cold ground.

Many squirrels sleep all winter, but others are up and about. Often a squirrel will build a nest in a hollow tree and fill it with twigs and dry leaves. Many tiny openings in the nest make it light and fluffy. When the squirrel curls up, the heat from its body helps keep the nest warm.

As soon as it starts getting cold in the fall, the deer begins to shed its summer coat and begins to get a winter coat. Each hair of new this coat is hollow. The outer end is sealed. With this warm covering the deer needs no other shelter except when it is very cold; then the deer goes underneath a tree.

So let the winds blow and the snow fly. God has given winter's creatures many ways to keep cozy and warm.

# The Answer Was Golden

*A FICTION STORY*
*by Bernice Gregory*

Matt Andrews shut the chicken house door firmly and handed a pail of feed to his brother. Suddenly, he stopped.

"Look over there, Jon—by the shed," he whispered.

Jon looked around uncertainly, then grinned. "A dog, Matt! A real, live dog!"

"Sh-h-h, you might scare him away," his older brother warned.

"I wonder what's wrong with him?" Jon said. "He's just lying there."

They walked quietly across the yard, but the dog seemed too tired to move. A small pool of blood gathered in the dust by her front paw. The dog was covered with a thick layer of Texas dust, but underneath the boys could see a beautiful red coat.

"Matt," Jon said, "is this our answer to prayer?"

To have their own dog had been the boys' dream since they'd moved out to the farm. Their mom had wanted one too, but Dad had said they couldn't afford to feed a dog. So the boys had given up hope.

Then they had been invited to attend the little church down the road. There both boys had received Jesus as Saviour. Their mom soon saw such a difference in them that she started going to church too. Now they were all Christians—except Dad, who said, "I can take just as good care of myself as God can."

But the boys knew that wasn't so, for they now had a Heavenly Father who heard and answered prayer. Someday, they were sure God would answer their prayers for their dad and for a dog.

The dog whimpered a little and licked Matt's hand.

Jon stared in admiration. "I've never seen such silky fur on a dog, Matt. What kind of dog is it?"

"It's a red Irish setter," Matt answered. "Move over now so I can see what's wrong."

Matt ran his hands over the big dog's body. "She's got a bad leg, Jon," he said finally. "Must've torn it on some barbed wire. Let's get her some water."

Hurriedly, Jon filled a can nearby with some water and held it under the dog's muzzle so she could drink. The setter began lapping it up.

"I thought I sent you boys to—" Suddenly the booming voice above them stopped. "Well, I'll be. Where did the dog come from, boys?" their dad asked.

"We just found her lying here by the shed," Matt explained.

Dad gently ran his hands over the quivering dog. "She's a fine animal, boys," he said. "But that doesn't mean we can keep her. She looks like a show dog to me. Someone's probably hunting for her right now. Besides, she's going to have pups soon. That makes her even more valuable."

"But if no one claims her, can we have her, Dad?" Matt

asked.

"We'll see, Son. She's a big dog and big dogs eat a lot. But for now, take her up to the house and bandage that leg. Ask Mom to feed her. I'll go over to Brown's and see if they've heard anything about a lost dog. I'll try the gas station down the road too.

"Let's call her 'Red Girl,' Matt," Jon suggested as they helped the setter along the path to the house.

"Well, I see we have a guest," Mom greeted them. "Bring her in. She looks tired and needs a good cleaning up."

Matt cleaned and bandaged the dog's wound while Jon warmed up some leftovers Mom gave him. The dog ate hungrily, careful to clean up any food that spilled.

When Dad came in, Red Girl thumped her shaggy tail in greeting. He scratched her ears and Matt and Jon grinned at each other. Maybe if Dad liked her enough. . . .

"Well," Dad began, "no one seems to have heard of a lost dog. It looks like we'll have to keep her for a couple of days until we find out where she's from."

That night Matt prayed, "Please, God, let this dog be the one we've asked You for. Don't let anyone come for her."

But he suddenly realized he was praying selfishly. Maybe even now Red Girl's owner was praying for her return.

"I'm sorry I said that, God," he whispered. "If it's Your will to let us keep her, I'd sure be happy. But if not, I'll understand."

The next morning he woke up to find Jon shaking him excitedly. "Come quick, Matt. Hurry!"

Matt raced for the kitchen. Then he stopped short, his mouth open in amazement. There, in a big, quilt-lined box lay Red Girl proudly washing four puppies—three red and one golden.

**110**

The boys took to the little golden pup right away. "See, Dad," Jon said. "We prayed for one dog and Jesus sent us five!"

Dad shook his head. "We might have kept one dog, boys, but five is out of the question."

But for several weeks they did have five dogs. Dad continued to make inquiries, but no one had heard of a missing red setter.

Then one afternoon while the boys were playing with the pups, a big car drove up to the house. The man who got out wore expensive clothes.

"Hello, Mr. Andrews," he called when Dad came out. "I'm John DeGraff. The gas station owner told me you have a dog here that sounds like the one I'm looking for—a red Irish setter, female."

Dad nodded. "Pleased to meet you, Mr. DeGraff. Matt, bring Red Girl and the pups."

The man smiled. "So the pups got here all right, did they? She seemed to be having a hard time at first, and I was taking her to the vet in Bradford. But while I was in a restaurant, someone took her right out of the car. I didn't know which way they'd taken her, but she must have gotten away from them."

"Well, that explains why a fine dog like her was just roaming around," Dad replied.

Jon crouched down by Red Girl and stroked her. "Matt," he whispered, his voice trembling, "let's turn the pups loose and say they ran away."

Matt put his arm around his younger brother. "We're Christians now, Jon. God doesn't want us to lie."

Slowly, each boy picked up two puppies and walked to the house with Red Girl at their heels.

At the sight of her, Mr. DeGraff leaned over and

stretched out his arms, "Here, Princess," he called.

Like lightning the big setter flashed past the boys, up the path, and into the man's arms.

"I certainly owe you a debt of gratitude for taking such good care of Princess," the man said, reaching for his wallet.

Dad waved the money aside. "We don't want money for being hepful, Mr. DeGraff. Your dogs have given the boys lots of pleasure."

The boys put the squirming pups down. "Good-bye, Red Girl," Jon said. Then he patted the golden puppy. "And good-bye, Golden."

The man looked at the dogs and then at the boys. Then he turned to the mother dog. "Well, now, look what you went and did, Princess," he said, grinning. "You know I can't have anything but red dogs in my kennel, so I guess Golden is just going to have to stay if these folks will let him."

Matt and Jon looked at Dad and he nodded. But before they could say thanks, the man whisked Princess and the other puppies to his car. He got in, waved to them, and drove off.

"Mom, look!" Jon cried as his mother came out of the house. "We thought Red Girl was the dog God sent us, but Golden was instead."

Mom smiled. "The Lord has His own way of answering our prayers, Son."

Dad scratched Golden under the chin. "Well, pup," he said softly, "if God sent you, I guess it's up to us to take care of you."

# Little Cheese Thief

*by Gloria A. Truitt*

I'm a little rodent with
   Soft fur of brown or gray.
My tail is long and slender and
   In fields I live and play.

If Mom should catch a glimpse of me
   Scampering 'cross a room,
She'll probably try to swat me with
   Her handy, kitchen broom.

I'll surely steal your cheese if I
   Should get inside your house;
For I'm that clever rascal who
   Is simply called a mouse!

# Where's Buttercup?

## A TRUE STORY
### by Ann Snider

*This summer sure is warm!* Jennifer Vincent decided as she lay stretched out under the old maple trees by the farmhouse. The shade of the large trees gave welcome relief from July's sticky heat.

Jennifer glanced at the new watch she'd just received for her 12th birthday. *Time to round up the cows for milking.*

But where was their collie, Zero? He and Ebony always helped her herd the cattle. Jennifer could see Ebony standing under the elm tree in the barnyard beside the water trough. But Zero was not in sight.

She gathered up her blanket, empty lemonade glass, and book and put them on the porch. Then she whistled for Zero. But the large golden collie failed to respond. *He's probably hiding in the barn,* Jennifer said to herself, and called him again and again.

Finally, she walked over to Ebony. "Guess it's up to you and me to bring the cattle home today," she told the horse. "But I won't saddle you. It's too hot for that. Just move over here by the fence so I can get up on you. That's a girl!"

Jennifer settled onto Ebony's broad back and gave Zero one last call. When he didn't appear, she and Ebony trotted down the lane toward the fields behind the barn.

*Finding the cows won't be easy either*, Jennifer thought. *No doubt they're hiding in the shade of scrub trees in the swale.\* It will take a lot of coaxing to get them out.*

She had guessed correctly. Now that it was late afternoon, some cattle were standing near the pond. Others were grouped in the shade of the woods. A few were scattered here and there under trees around the swamp.

Jennifer slid off Ebony. The horse knew what to do. She trotted around the stragglers and headed them in the direction of the barn while Jennifer chased out the few in the swale and pond.

"I wish Zero had come," she muttered to herself as she waded through the long grass and thickets, shuddering over the thought of possible, slithering snakes. Zero would bound in and out of the thicket, nipping the heels of dawdling cows and yapping mercilessly until all the cattle were gathered up and headed onto the main path.

After half an hour of running in and out of the brush, yelling and throwing clumps of dirt in her frustration, Jennifer finally had the herd plodding in an orderly fashion on the trail toward home.

She caught up to Ebony and gave a quick count: "One, two, three . . .forty-four! Great! One missing." She looked them over carefully. "Of course, it's Buttercup!"

Buttercup was a golden Jersey cow, a family pet. She

---

*Swale—a low-lying, wet area that is often overgrown with willows and dwarf trees.

had caused excitement a number of times in the past. As far as Jennifer could tell, Buttercup had the best memory of any cow in the herd. First day out in the field in the spring, she would head for a hole in the fence that she remembered from the fall before. She was a nosey animal too and would snoop into anything that looked unusual.

Since Ebony was taking the cattle by the main farm lane that skirted the swale, maybe she could take the cow path through the middle and catch up with them on the barn side. Jennifer picked her way carefully through the thick brush, trying not to get her feet wet in the soggy marsh. She had to watch for the boggy areas that were like quicksand.

It sure was hot! Deer flies kept biting her in hard to reach places, and she tried not to listen for sounds of slithering things.

Buttercup was nowhere to be seen. Jennifer was almost hoarse from calling, "Co-boss!" She heard no answering "moo," only the buzzing of disturbed mosquitoes.

Back in the farmyard at last, Jennifer was glad to see that her father and Howard, the hired man, were back with their last load of hay. She left Ebony and the cattle grouped around the watering troughs and went into the barn where Zero greeted her with a guilty look and an apologetic tail wag.

"Zero, where were you?" Jennifer cried. "You old lazy bones—I needed your help. I probably would have found Buttercup if you had been along." But she gave him a forgiving pat, and together they climbed up to the main floor where the two men were unloading the last of the day's hay.

"Dad, all the cows are here except Buttercup. I walked through the swale, thinking I would find her."

"Well, Pumpkin," her father said, "don't worry about it.

She's been around long enough to know it's milking time. With all the other cattle gone, she'll give up hiding soon and show up for milking."

But Buttercup wasn't at the gate at milking time, and she wasn't there when chores were done and it was too late to search for her. Nor was she there in the morning.

Family prayers after breakfast included concern for Buttercup. Dad read the Bible story about the woman who lost a coin, searched for it till it was found, then invited friends in to rejoice with her. Jennifer wondered if God was interested in helping them find a lost Jersey cow.

"Jennifer, you saddle up Ebony and ride through the woods!" Dad directed. "Howard, you check the island. Maybe Buttercup broke through the fence and wandered over there on the causeway. I'll have a look through the swale. She might have wandered off the main path. There are some pretty bad places in there."

Jennifer's heart skipped a beat. She knew now what her dad was thinking. All those soft spots that jiggled like jello underfoot. If a heavy cow broke through. . . . Jennifer didn't want to think about what could happen.

The woods were cool and fragrant. Jennifer, riding Ebony and followed by Zero, took each path that wound around the woods. Ordinarily, Jennifer would take her time in the welcome cool of the woods, but not today. Buttercup *had* to be found. Jennifer saw plenty of animals—small ones—birds too. But no Buttercup.

Just as the three were emerging from the woods, Jennifer heard a shrill whistle. Dad must have found Buttercup! Jennifer goaded Ebony into a gallop, and with Zero racing behind, headed for the swale. Howard was running across the fields.

At the swale, Jennifer halted Ebony and called, "Where

are you, Dad?" She listened. His whistle came again from a section of the swamp she had not been through. She slid off Ebony. It would be impossible to ride her horse into the dense brush.

Howard arrived then, huffing and puffing. Without a word, both Howard and Jennifer plunged through the thicket and followed a narrow trail. They soon had to slow down as their feet began to sink into the soupy clay. With each step, their boots threatened to pull off.

"Don't come any farther!" Jennifer heard her dad call. "We'll need help." Jennifer peered through the shrubs, looking for Buttercup. Dad was perched on the lower limb of an old tree.

"Jennifer, go back to the house," her dad ordered. "Have Mom call the vet and a few neighbors. Howard, please bring the tractor and wagon back. And we'll need some wide planks, rope, shovels, and axes—maybe the chain saw too. We must hurry if we are to save her."

Jennifer heard a sucking sound. Between the branches of the brush, two frightened eyes stared up at her. Buttercup had struggled against the bog only to be sucked deeper into the mire. Just her head remained above the wet, spongy earth.

"Buttercup!" Jennifer cried with a sob.

The cow didn't move. She just snorted faintly. A few more inches and she would sink beneath the gray-green bog.

Jennifer tried to run, but the ground sucked at her feet as if it wanted to swallow her too. "Jennifer, don't run," Howard called out as he stumbled along behind her. "Watch out for soft spots!"

But all she could see were Buttercup's terror-stricken eyes and muddied face.

Jennifer and Howard reached Ebony at the same time. "For speed's sake, I'd better ride Ebony too," he said. He swung into the saddle and pulled Jennifer up behind him. Ebony galloped full speed all the way to the farmhouse.

Zero did not follow. He had gotten in close to Buttercup and had laid down next to her, whining anxiously as if to comfort her.

Jennifer was the first to return. Over one shoulder she had slung a thick rope. She was dragging a shovel behind her with the other hand. Her father had thrown a rotting log on top of the muck and was now balancing on it.

"Good—throw me that rope," he called when he saw Jennifer. He caught it and wound it around the tree's lower limb. The other end he wound around himself, then inched his way across the log toward Buttercup.

"Throw me that shovel!" he called.

Jennifer heaved it to him as best she could.

Cautiously, Dad began to dig around Buttercup's neck and shoulders.

"What are you doing, Dad?" she asked. The water and muck seemed to fill in as fast as he dug.

"I'm trying to clear her shoulders. If we can get a rope in under her front legs, maybe we can pull her out."

The sound of the tractor and men's voices grew louder. Then what a hive of activity that corner of the swamp became! Men chopped at bushes in their way. Large planks were thrown over the top of the bog near Buttercup. Men surrounded the cow, balancing on the planks and working with shovels. But the wet earth seemed determined to hold Buttercup forever.

They had cleared a path for the tractor. Howard steered it in as close as he could on firm ground. Ropes were shoved through the muck and behind Buttercup's front

**119**

legs, then inched along until they were centered under her middle. Now she came to life, struggling and bellowing in panic.

Jennifer kept telling herself to close her eyes and pray as the tractor began to pull—but she just had to watch.

She was so absorbed in Buttercup's struggle that she did not notice Doc Rob's arrival until she heard him mutter, "Well, I'll be!"

With great shouts of encouragement and the extra pull from the tractor, Buttercup was half-dragged, half-lifted to firmer ground where she finally stood trembling from exhaustion and fear.

Jennifer was startled to hear Doc Rob chuckle. "In all my years, I've never seen such a sight," he said.

The gray clay of the swamp was caked all over Buttercup. Only her head gave any hint of her normal Jersey gold. She and the weary clay-spattered men around her looked like unfinished clay figurines!

"Well, Mr. Vincent," Doc Rob shouted above the roar of the tractor, "she doesn't appear to be suffering from much more than embarrassment!"

It was true. In spite of overwhelming weariness, it was obvious that Buttercup was embarrassed. Jennifer went up and gently scratched the cow's muddied face. "Never mind, Buttercup. I'm so glad we found you. When you get back into your stall, I'll clean you up and soon no one will ever know what happened."

Jennifer put her arms around the cow's clay-caked neck while Doc Rob examined Buttercup's legs and forequarters where the rope had pulled. He did not find any serious injuries but said he would give the cow a closer look once she was in her stall.

The strange procession of clay cow and men and tractor headed back to the farm. In spite of all the noisy talk and laughter and the tractor's roar, Jennifer remembered the morning's prayers for Buttercup's safety and whispered her thanks to God for helping them find and rescue their wayward cow.

# Boots

*A FICTION STORY*
*by Esther L. Vogt*

"Boots, you stay right here!" Heidi Mason cried, picking up her black cat and cuddling it in her arms. "You know what happens when you scoot down these stairs and out into the street. Please don't run away again."

"Cats can't understand," Heidi's 16-year-old brother Tim said. "I don't see why you had to drag that cat along to this apartment. Mr. Anderson was kind enough to let us live up here since Dad—" Tim's gruff voice trailed off.

It was true. Daddy had worked in the shipping room of Anderson's Department store for years. Then suddenly he had died, and the Masons were forced to sell their house near the park.

Mr. Anderson had kindly offered the small apartment above one corner of the store to the three of them: Mom, Tim, and Heidi. He also gave Tim a job after school as a cleanup man in the display windows. And Mom got a night job at a nearby hospital.

Of course, Mr. Anderson didn't know about Boots. And

**122**

Tim worried that he'd find out. But Heidi was lonely. She felt God had sent Boots to her for company since she had to be alone a lot now. She promised there would be no trouble.

"There'd better not be," Tim growled again, and left to go down to clean up a display window. Heidi settled down on the couch with her homework, and Boots purred contentedly beside her.

When Heidi finished her math, she reached over to pick up her cat. He was gone! She quickly searched the small apartment but Boots wasn't *anywhere*!

Tim walked in minutes later. "Whew! What a job! The window display manager has fixed the window up like a classy living room with dummies dressed in nice clothes, sitting in red velvet chairs. I tried not to mess anything up. Hey, Heidi, you're not even listening. Anything wrong?"

"It's Boots," she said sadly. "He's gone. Just disappeared!"

Tim sighed. "Cats have a way of showing up when they're ready," he said. "You'll see. By morning, he'll be back."

Before going to bed Heidi asked God to help her find Boots. "Tomorrow's Saturday. I'll watch him better," she promised.

But in the morning there was no sign of Boots—until Tim slammed in again from downstairs. He was carrying the black cat.

"Heidi!" he yelled. "You'd better watch your cat or you'll lose him. Know where he was?"

Heidi had hurried into the kitchen and taken Boots into her arms. "O Boots, where were you?"

"Guess," Tim said mysteriously. "When I went down to the Center Street window for a quick look, people were crowded in front of it—laughing and talking and pointing. Then I saw *your* cat in the lap of one of the mannequins, washing his face.

"About that time Mr. Anderson came along and saw what was going on. He went to his office and pushed every button on his desk. When we rushed in, he roared, 'Why is that cat in the Center Street window? He's sitting on one of our finest dresses, licking himself!' "

"O Boots!" Heidi cried. "You didn't!"

"Yes, he *did*," Tim said. "When the janitor and I opened the door to the window, that cat jumped out and raced to the back of the store. Luckily Mr. Anderson didn't find out whose cat it was, because he was *really* mad."

Heidi nodded dumbly. She would have to keep a closer watch on Boots. Tomorrow was Sunday and Tim wouldn't need to go down to the store.

On Monday night when Tim went down to clean the Walsh Street window, he hollered for Heidi to keep the apartment door closed.

"Of course, I will," she answered. She would make sure that Boots couldn't possibly leave the apartment.

But when Heidi was ready to put Boots to bed, the cat was nowhere to be found. How *could* he have gotten out? Maybe Tim was right. Maybe she shouldn't have brought Boots to the apartment.

When Heidi came home from school the next afternoon, Boots waited for her on the couch. She scooped him up in her arms as Mom came into the room.

"Tim says Boots was in the Walsh Street window this morning. It was furnished to look like a bedroom—thick rugs and all. A large sign on the bed said: SLEEP LIKE A KITTEN, and there lay Boots!"

Heidi couldn't help but smile. "What did Mr. Anderson

say this time?" she asked.

Mom shook her head. "He said that something would have to be done about that cat, if he only knew whose it was."

When Tim came in, he grabbed Heidi's arm roughly. "Look, Heidi, we're going to have to get rid of that crazy cat. He's followed me twice into the show windows at night. Mr. Anderson is awfully upset, and I could lose my job when he finds out it's our cat!"

Heidi went along when Tim went down to clean the second window on Walsh Street to make sure Boots didn't follow them in.

Before she left for school the next day, she ran downstairs and out into the street. She saw a crowd in front of the Market Street window which had been fixed to look like an outdoor scene, with rocks and a tree and a clear pool with real fish. There were fishing rods, creels, hip boots—everything a sportsman needed to go fishing. Near the pool a sign said: HAVE THE TIME OF YOUR LIFE FISHING!

Heidi almost choked when she saw Boots sitting on a branch, then cavorting around the tree. When he put his paw into the pool to catch a fish, people in the front of the window screamed with laughter.

Just then Mr. Anderson came up. He took one look and stalked into his store. Heidi's heart sank. "Dear God," she whispered, "I guess You didn't want me to keep Boots after all."

Instead of going to school, Heidi walked slowly into the store and to Mr. Anderson's office. It was time he learned the facts.

As she neared Mr. Anderson's office, she heard him shout, "I want that cat out of that window. Get rid of it once and for all!"

The manager cleared his throat. "But Mr. Anderson, since that cat has been in our show windows, our sales have nearly doubled!"

"What?" Mr. Anderson roared, and Heidi trembled as she stepped forward.

"Mr.—Mr. Anderson, I'm Heidi Mason. The cat is mine. How Boots gets into the store windows is a mystery. We live upstairs—"

Heidi moved nearer his desk. "Please, Mr. Anderson, Boots is very dear to me, but I don't want Tim to lose his job. You can do with Boots—"

Just then the phone rang, and Mr. Anderson answered it. "Yes? Oh, from the *Daily Globe*? You say the whole town's talking about our trained cat? Why, yes, I guess that could be arranged. No. No trouble at all. Good-bye."

Mr. Anderson grinned at Heidi and said, "You think a lot of your brother, don't you? More than of the cat? Well, don't worry about Tim's job."

Then he turned to the store manager and said, "Listen, have somebody go get that cat. The *Daily Globe* wants a picture of him. Let's see. In which window should we put our 'trained' cat tomorrow?"

"THE BASEMENT IS FLOODED AGAIN."

# Lester Adopts a Family

### A FICTION STORY
### by Grace Fox Anderson

David Lewis sat bolt upright in bed. Something had awakened him. But what? An occasional car passed on the highway in front of his grandparents' place and a bullfrog "kerwunked" out on the large duck pond. But that's all.

Then he heard muffled voices and shuffling feet—probably Grandpa moving down the hall. Had something awakened him too?

David got up and looked out of his back window. A yard light flooded the patio but didn't reach as far as the pond. The chickens were restless, but they did fuss at night sometimes, he'd discovered.

Someone walked onto the patio then, and the 10-year-old boy jumped. But it was only Grandpa.

David leaned out of the window. "What's wrong, Grandpa?" he called.

Grandpa whirled around and saw David. "I don't know. Thought I heard something, but guess not."

David shrugged and crawled back into bed—but not to

sleep. Instead, his mind began to churn over the events of the past weeks. He still couldn't believe that his mother was dead—killed in a car accident just five weeks ago.

Why had God let her die? She was a believer in Jesus Christ and a great mother. David and Dad were believers too, but it seemed as if God had deserted them.

Now David was staying in Kentucky with his grandparents for a few weeks while Dad was on a business trip. But fishing in the pond and laughing at the antics of the ducks and geese and chickens only sometimes eased the pain in his heart. Then he'd start thinking about Mom again.

Would he ever feel whole or really happy again? Would he ever again feel like trusting God?

Eventually, David fell asleep to be awakened by bright sunshine and the smell of bacon and coffee. He hurried into his clothes and out to the kitchen.

Gram was just pulling a pan of biscuits from the oven. "Will you set the table, please, David?" she asked.

"Sure," he said. He was getting used to household chores now that he and Dad were alone.

Just then he noticed that Grandpa wasn't there reading his newspaper. "Where's Grandpa?" he asked.

"I'm afraid something sad has happened," Gram told him. "Last night we thought we heard gunshots. This morning Grandpa found two of the geese had been killed. He's burying them now."

"No kidding?" David gasped. "Who would do that?"

"I can't imagine," Gram said. "Killing someone's pets just for 'the fun of it' is pure cruelty."

Grandpa came in then, looking like a thunder cloud. "What gets into people?" he growled. "Maybe liquor. What else? Everyone around here knows that's our pond and the critters are tame."

David especially enjoyed the pair of white geese—Lily and Lester. On water they looked as graceful as swans, but on land they walked like bowlegged cowboys. "Which ones were killed?" he asked.

Grandpa shook his head. "Would you believe they got old Sam, the Canada goose—and Lily?"

"Oh, no, Grandpa!" David exclaimed. "Is Lester OK?"

Grandpa nodded. "I can't figure out how he escaped. He and Lily were inseparable. He's wandering around like a lost soul since I buried Lily and Sam."

Gram brought the food to the table, but none of them were very hungry. When they'd finished breakfast, Grandpa reached for the Bible.

"Honey, why don't you read those verses from Matthew 10 about the sparrows," Gram suggested.

Grandpa nodded, found the place, and read, " 'Are not two sparrows sold for a penny? Yet not one of them will fall to the ground apart from the will of your Father. And even the very hairs of your head are all numbered. So don't be afraid; you are worth more than many sparrows' " (Matt. 10:29-30, NIV).

David thought about those verses as he walked around the pond to see where Grandpa had buried the geese. So God said He *did* care about him and Dad—even knew how many hairs they had! "Thank You, Lord, for loving us—even though Mom is gone," he prayed.

Lester came waddling after him, and David turned to pat the big goose on the neck. "Sorry, old boy," he said to Lester. "I hope you don't feel as sad about Lily as I do about Mom. But from what Grandpa read this morning, God even cares about geese."

Just then the two children from next door—Kevin, six, and his four-year-old sister Mary—came running up. "Did you see the ducklings?" Kevin cried.

"They're so cute!" Mary squealed.

Kevin and Mary always seemed to show up when David most wanted to be alone. But Kevin's news was exciting since they'd all been waiting for this particular duck to hatch her eggs. She had chosen an unprotected spot in the yard to sit on them, so Grandpa had built a pen around her.

"Well, what are we waiting for? Let's go see them," David said, and off they ran with Lester waddling along behind.

When they arrived, huffing and puffing, Grandpa was taking down the chicken-wire pen. Gram was there too.

David grinned when he saw the little balls of colored fluff. "They sure are cute," he said.

"Nothing sweeter than baby ducks," Gram agreed.

"Just hope we don't lose too many to snapping turtles and snakes," Grandpa said.

"There's 12 of them," Kevin said, counting. "All different colors!"

Mother Duck seemed delighted to be out of her pen. Right away, she led her ducklings to the pond.

"The babies can swim!" Mary cried as the ducklings followed Mother Duck into the water.

"And there goes Lester into the water after them," said Kevin.

"Looks more like he's rounding up the ducklings," Gram said.

"Maybe he'll adopt them," Grandpa suggested, chuckling.

"Would he do that?" David asked.

"We'll see," Grandpa said.

And they certainly did see, for from that day on, Lester followed the duck family everywhere they went. What a funny sight to see only the head and neck of the tall, white bodyguard moving through the long grass that completely hid the ducks. And if other geese or ducks got too close, Lester went after them, honking loudly.

One day while David was helping Gram in the garden, they got to talking about how Lester had solved his problem with loneliness. "It almost seems like God sent the ducklings along just when Lester needed them, doesn't it, Gram?" David observed.

Gram looked up from her weeding. "I wouldn't put it past the Lord. You know He cares for the smallest creature. And there's nothing like helping others to take your mind off your own troubles."

Just then Kevin and Mary came and begged David to come play. He was going to say no, then saw the sad looks on their faces. "Is it all right, Gram?" he asked.

"You go ahead," Gram said, nodding.

"Let's look at the ducks first," Kevin cried, running toward the pond.

The ducklings were lying in the sun with their mother—under Lester's watchful eyes. "See, they're all there," Kevin added as he counted again. "I bet by now, Grandpa Lewis would have lost some if it hadn't been for Lester."

David laughed. "He makes a pretty good guard goose, all right."

When the children giggled, David thought, *I guess God sent me some "ducklings" to take care of too.*

Aloud, he challenged, "Race you to your swings. Last one there is a big fat goose!"

Winner Books are produced by Victor Books and are designed to entertain and instruct young readers in Christian principles.

**Other Winner Books you will enjoy:**